YEAR OF THE RAT

YEAR OF THE RAT

MARC ANTHONY
RICHARDSON

FC2
TUSCALOOSA

Death and life are in the power of the tongue: and
they that love it shall eat the fruit thereof.
—Proverbs 18:21

YEAR OF THE RAT

PALUS EPIDEMIARIUM

FOR SHE HAD JUST WHISKED AWAY the white sheet that was covering the red clay corpse and was now standing in the swelter of the hospital house with those eyes rising to rivet the soulless holes of the doctor's—she ain't dead, she said, she ain't dead, wake her up: my mother is dead. Died in nineteen forty-nine. Down in the red claylands of the southern savanna. She died on a table turned into a gurney by being fastened with four fast wheels to serve the orifices of Thanatos, and *the family that eats together stays together* comes to mind whenever my mother my malady—my mother is dead. Died at four and a half. Hit by a motorcar. Wild as she was she had run too far—so when it tore around the bend it threw her off a red dirt road into a red clay ditch which caught her like a mitt; the driver kept going, dust cleared, he was white as white as a ghost the driver, so when he kept going he disappeared and my mother all dusty and shadowy in the red clay ditch was so scared she fell asleep: a man with a mule saw it all. The white pall would fall. And in would storm the storm into that hospital house, whites stopping my nana, telling her her daughter is dead, hit by a motorcar, brought in with a broken clavicle and leg and a nasty blow to the head, so she's dead, says the doctor and nurse, she is gone, untethered from us to tumble about on a tumultuous sea for coloreds and they cannot get her back—so that's when Nana at five-foot-two with a sepia hue and the high chiseled cheekbones of a Blackfoot pushes them apart, the doctor and nurse, pushes them both apart as if together they are a curtain of white and marches straight back into that emergency room, a kitchen, to behold the large maple dining table fastened with four fast wheels and covered with cotton matting to serve up the fresh course of a dead pickaninny, and then bumps aside the nurse who has just placed the wet white pall over the small and broken body and throws it back so fast that it whips and turns the *nurse's* cheek, so that the blood of two could be on this sheet; she ain't dead, she says, turning to face the doctor who's hurried in after her, wake her up, she says in a low and even tone, punching the soulless holes out of the back of his head with her eyes and I can smell the smell of my mother's water pipes having released full strength, I can see the eyes of my nana clenching the tissue of one dead child already, her second born my would-be uncle's body, I can feel her eyes jolting the doctor's scruples, driving nail-like into that thick bias in him the stark probability of his purple mortality; so without further ado, while pinching closed the little nose, this bigot puts his mouth onto my mother's mouth, as tiny as it is (Nana looking onward in shock, I'm sure, containing herself barely), and then rises and presses down on that tiny chest cavity with a tentative yet resolved palm to return to that mouth-to-mouth, alternating the two until at last, like a golden apple chunk, out comes my mother's shadow and she is breathing again.

Except this isn't what happened at all, *the truth is not distorted here but rather a certain distortion is used to get at the truth,*[1] for when my nana told the doctor to wake her daughter up he did nothing, he did absolutely nothing, so she just prayed. All she had to do was plead the blood of the lamb and that was it that was that, and since my mother had lived nearly nine years into the new millennium, as to whether or not I could swallow this didn't make any difference now did it, sick women live forever. She had been living her death her entire life. For that eighth year into the new millennium, her last year alive, inside a one-bedroom apartment her thirty-five-year-old son had since resumed his role in her perpetual teleplay: the program of a sixty-three-year-old woman whom he'd never known without a malady; the mind had been reared for it. Outside snow and inside a gated community, a stasis a stoppage of the bodily fluids for the crippled and the decrepit and for the offspring they'd taken in to take care of them, I was sharing with her a folie à deux a madness of two, for lunar New Year, year of the rat, I ended up holding her half-naked body in the dark while we writhed in wavelengths from the heavens, washed aglow by death throes and the hottest evolution of the television.

Nearby: bedlam, the northern section of this city this northern city, a blight of municipality where deadly caprice and cul-de-sacs form a fearful symmetry, and where all hell breaks loose and niggers hate nothing more or quite as much as themselves. Although there are the museums, the Rodin and that widely held and most muscular *Thinker*, gardener of thought of minotaur of thought (where is the now? where is the now?), those lively and maggoty *Gates of Hell*, and those large immutable extremities of that slightly larger-than-life sextuplet of dribbling aqua-discolored candles of ghoulish altruism, *The Burghers of Calais;* and down the Parkway towards the city's center is the Academy of Art and Museum, my raison d'être at the time, for I had already completed a year in a four-year curriculum. However that winter, due to an anarchic inability to support myself, I had to suspend studious leisure to revert to work to return to my studies in the fall: it was a long shot, I knew, but with a traveling fellowship I could tour another countryside, sharpen my eye widen my mind whet my palate inside a Florentine atelier as a painter's apprentice, to buy my mother away someday from here without compromising the vision. For two years earlier I had motored across this country from the Pacific to the Atlantic, towards the Northern East, towards a grim and crumpling armpit of a city a beautiful gray city where beauty is earned and eaten like a little bit of bread, whose colonial streets and segregated neighborhoods look like tombs or as though bombs and homegirls and hand grenades had blown away gaps in the mortar the memory, towards this birthplace of freedom; however after the stabilization of her post-brain-tumor behavior I undertook the traumatic return to the golden Pacific, some three thousand miles once more to my love my rib my Medusa Marie—yet in less than a month back out west I would relinquish the auto to hurl myself deeper into an already-catastrophic debt, to be flown home once compunction precluded a separate existence: being away from the mother's maladies made me feel as though my love my rib my Medusa Marie could be pulled out from under me, and I was wholly made of doubt and glass.

So that now she sought the sufferer's bliss: a medical miracle in the making or some dietary undertaking, smoother than all the rest, but one shouldn't hope for the best in substitute spread if one has already risen from the dead, thrice for three sons, one shouldn't hope for a miracle if one is a symptom of god. So: she subsisted. Sick women live forever. Even her brain knew the backwardness of this since that doctor had discovered its protest encysted in it, the meningioma tumor; she had to tap her skull, the doc, had to crack her head open with an electric saw in order to scoop it out, and so our foreheads had matching dents: mine from falling down as an adolescent and hers from falling apart as an adult—yet I knew I knew I threw myself beneath those wheels, the devastating wait, the wait for some kind of culmination; time and time again I had participated in idolatry, the worshiping of suffering; everyday I flung my bones under the crushing credence of that five-foot-two two-hundred-and-seventy-so-pound Jagannatha, for it was never simply about giving things up or restraining myself against destructive pleasures, those things that were done to regain good grace were only stones building up the altar, not the sacrifice. I surrendered to her body because it wasn't dead, that's why I'm here, I thought, because it isn't dead, so I decided to wake it up—but the clue as to how the hell I was supposed to do this eluded me, because in a benign state I had made the mistake of asking her to write down all her illnesses all her surgeries, everything that has ever happened to her, hoping I could help her hoping I could figure her out. And she did. Write it all down. A table of contents:

I. illnesses i'm treated for by uncle sam he pay for
   1. hip and thigh sprain
   2. lumbar disc hernia (my back)
   3. nervous disorder (my legs)
   4. depression

II. i also have
   5. insomnia
   6. high colesterol
   7. high blood pressure
   8. anjá pictoris (my heart)
   9. allergies
   10. irregular breathing
   11. bad bladder control
   12. chronic constipation
   13. diabetes (lost all my teeth)
   14. operations
     a. head
       i. broke by a motorcar
       ii. mengeoma tumor (my brain)
     b. neck
       i. thyroid
     c. collarbones
       i. broke by a motorcar
       ii. broke by a baseball
     d. eye
       i. diabetic retinal (my right eye)
       ii. cataracts (both eyes)

e. leg and knee
   i. left leg broke by a motorcar
   ii. right knee replaced
f. ankles
   i. calcium deposit (too much in my body)
g. wrist
   i. carpal tunnel (my left)
h. stomach
   i. partial hysterectomy
   ii. full hysterectomy, one week later i laughed too hard
      and my bowels and intestines come out, took a long
      time to heal
   iii. infected ovary six months after that, my cootie cat
      smelled bad that's how i known
   iv. scar tissues removed from that operation a year later
   v. bad needled injection for diabetes, gangrene set in
      and had to have a chunk of my stomach tooken out
      the size of a grapefruit, stomach left open to heal
      from inside out for a year
i. back
   i. slipped disc L5-S1 (removed but not replaced)

III. births

had three sons, the first in '67 the second in '69 and you in
'72. you was the hardest and didn't want to come and had
to pay for you. you was suppose to be the girl and after you
the tubes was tied.

IV. migraines

had cluster migraines from 14 to 33. lost my lives to them
at least two times i could remember that put me in hospital of overdose, one by the doctors and one by myself.

i was give so much medicine and even morphine needled myself. but i died at 4½. the doctor pronounced me dead and ever since i been walking.

We die only once, and for such a long time.[2] For every day she took a paragraph of pills and peed on herself still, took a handful of, let's say, ten twenty pills at a time and just gulped them down. And on a routine basis near the sciatic she had steroids stabbed into her spine and behind the oft-ice-packed caps of her knees, because ever since she was dis-eased, ever since she was tainted by her first quietus, she had been in such varying degrees of pain and impediment that her footfalls, itty-bitty as they were, had stretched infinitely beyond her years. And she was so nice, never spleeny or whiny, she was so fucking long-suffering it made me sick, and just like a mama bird she would not only give you the food off her plate but off her palate, just regurgitate the goop into the gullet. She'd give you her damn dentures if she thought you needed them because deep down down deep she lacked facility, she lacked the ability to explore her unexplained selves, her terra incognita if you will, lost it a long time ago when she married my father, the pawn of his pain—yet she was the pawn of her own. She was a damn hero and like most heroes she was only fulfilled in a proud modality of dying because she had lacked the ability to lose herself through verse form or craft: *All heroism expiates—by the genius of the heart—a defaulting talent; every hero is a being without talent; a man eliminates himself from the rank of his kind by the monastery or some other artifice—by morphine masturbation or rum—whereas a form of expression might have saved him.*[3]

LACUS OBLIVIONIS

WHERE IS THE NOW? where is the now? for I have looked up the word redundancy and it says *see redundant*. The Academy, the two-century-year-old school of art and museum, the first in the country, is right in front of me again and I have only two seasons to return; however due to the completion of a bygone degree and debt-doubling interest, exacerbated by all the lowly paying positions I had procured thereafter in great exquisite cities, by my habitual neglect, I am no longer eligible for anymore godsend; I have a partial scholarship but the other part needs tending to, so with the bank report having reached the nadir of a negative status, since it is early April, year of the rat, an unethical filing on the tax return is attempted—yet the accountant the aunt, the first of the seven sisters, just says you can't claim your mother as a dependent because she makes more than you.

Back in February I thought about getting a prominent position on a farm somewhere, some collective youth farm out there on the outskirts of here, for I have more than enough know-how, but the thought of traveling and working forty hours a week every single week, of becoming a seven-to-three or a three-to-eleven or an eleven-to-seven field hand farming beautifully fucked-up children inside an artificial environment, a non-home and then coming home to a non-home had made the decision for me: I would work with schoolchildren again. I started *shadowing*; no bosses (none on site), only one child to hold down (so I thought), and it pays more for fewer hours (not really)—ultimately I need to make the same or just about the same I would've made on a farm: I'm not trying to work more hours; drawing is more important. Although I need to amass the monies, although there is something a little bit perverse about shopping through a field that'll offer less hours (let alone utterly defeating the purpose), I need time to study by making just enough to stay sane, because after a week without creation—the antithesis of genesis—comes a nightfall of alcohol intake, of cavortingfightingfornicating and other fundamental merriments, so in the scraped-up face of dawn I take to shakes and shivers and cries into an enemy pillow, growing mossy with hate.

Yet the art is also under stress, for an illustrious illustration agent had told a promising illustrator that no one was going to pay him to be his own psychotherapist; she was referring to the unsavory content of his drawings, their lack of perspicuity and color, you say, she said, you only relish extremes, black

and white being inherently dramatic, but this won't help me
sell you; I like your drawings, I wouldn't have called you in if
I didn't, but you can be a little bit disturbing at times, a little
disagreeing. I disagree. *Good behavior is the last refuge of medioc-
rity,*[4] I said. Black and white can be the illustrator's best friend.
Color can compromise compassion. Color can rob integrity
of the real nitty-gritty and as far as working-my-own-shit-out-
through-my-work is concerned I am sorry, but drawing illustrations—especially for children—can be the most enriching
and disturbing thing for me: have you ever seen some of the
classical illustrations for Lewis Carroll's classic? However, I
didn't say, drawing disturbing images has never been so thera-
peutic as when I was antagonizing the police: I made them
once out west, those sirens of law, get out of their black-and-
white and kick my kidneys a couple of times just to get me to
get going, just to get me to stop doing what I was doing. I was
not sober. I was yelling I'm my father's son my father's son all
the way through, and afterwards every day for several days
it was just like I had crazy monkey sex: pissing sideways and
being prostrate or having poor posture and pain and I was suffering sirens. I was pissing blood. And let me assure you. The
sound is disagreeing.

It was a day! Bright and bold and demanding out when a
man asked me for spare change and I said none that I can spare
and kept walking: in the unseasonable heat of the week-long
arms of late March (cherry blossoms in premature bloom?) I
was en route to the Museum of Art when he hooked me, why
go to the same place, I thought, time and time again to revert to
drawing from the same lifeless piece of crap no matter how well-
lit well-done well-turned it is when you have flesh and emotion
and all the gorgeous angles of decadence right out in front of

you in the blazing sun, a scaffolded-for-scrubbing rejuvenated-marble-limestone-granite-divulging   laxative-colored-pigeon-pelted furnance-sooted coal-burnt railroad-blackened City Hall, a unique architectural achievement in the panache of the French Second Empire? Or a man in need of money like you? For food or folly—who cares? He's a grown man. So I went back and he asked why did you come back? Did he want five dollars? For what? To draw a portrait. How long did he have to sit? Four fifteen-minute sets or break at his leisure. He agreed. He was disagreeable. Drunk and drunk *I* grew drawing him—his breaths were like blows! He was a horrible sitter, kept dozing off. He thought it was going to be easy. I thought it was going to be easy, he said, but he had no idea how hard it is to sit still when you're conscious of it and toasted and when he said he was hungry that irritated the hell out of me, because before we started I had asked if he was and he said that he wasn't. He could quit if he wanted, three dollars if he stopped now. He said he wanted the full five. He'd hold out for the five. But the sun on the back of my neck was hot and on the page: I was sketching in the back of this blank book while sitting on this lightweight foldout stool I sometimes carry and every time I looked up to study him from that bleached white sheet of paper there'd be this dazzling impression where his face ought to be. It was an evil sketch. Not a good signature of his features at all. But somehow the way the sun shone and unshadowed us, the sense of a mother and child rear of me watching, the way the cherry blossoms posted petals on the breeze in a slanting showering grace, skimming our faces and skipping the walk, falling afoot over the shavings in the pencil kit was blamefully unforgettable. I stopped early and gave him the full five. I told him my name. He told me his. I'm looking at the drawing now.

There is something about spitting on a little girl that kind of sticks with you, for in the western section of this city, just last week, I was still assisting and assessing beautifully backward children in an asbestos-seething public school, an elementary school while working with a client, for he had become a shining candidate for a shadow (there are several in the room) after returning a girl's pencil—in the back—and gotten suspended only. I mean they could've kicked him out, but where was he going to go?: he's already at the bottom; he is like so many I've worked with: non-parented single-grandmothered sibling-severed little black bastards whose pretty long eyelashes are almost always disquieted and urban-curled with melancholy and grief. Big head-bloom of eyes he has too, makes you just want to go gobble-gobble and say sweet dreams you sweet sweet you. Sweet dreams. For near the school is the Cathedral Cemetery, Our Mother of Sorrows, as well as the family house with the grandmother and the seven brothers and a sister who, still a baby herself, had to abort one, the eldest brother's the absentee's the family's correctional limb's. Whenever I visited his house to get his blue-haired toxic-dust-induced-coughing grandmother and his rambling mobile therapist with his pinche Chihuahua nervousness and Morse code blinks to sign off on some documentation…I felt wrathful: in winter the house has icicles on the inside, in summer a ravenous humidity deflowers the petunia-patterned wallpaper (for the lower rooms have all been graced with the same dreariness of beautification), and the dining and living rooms have such massive water leaks from above that they'd permanently dried in the paper and plaster like two prehistoric progenies of the living fossil fish, the coelacanth, that had long crawled out of the dirty blue ocean of the ceiling to deliver the long and expensive history of the house's ineffective plumbing; perennially the place is a mess, loud and smelly and sardined with cousins and with the robust stench of noisy chunky dog shit shamelessly petrifying itself in the passerby's periphery; during hot musty nights relieved by bowling thunderstorms the house would be mercilessly breached by thumb-length waterbugs so plenteous that, upon edible unveilings, they would creep up from the crawl spaces cracks and crevices, from the porch the foundation the walkway adjacent the house to scurry up ankles so amorously that rubber bands are required around the pant cuffs of each and every family member. The whole sordid block is hanging on by sheer luck and a nail, both bent and oxidized and bubbling with tetanus, for right now a gust of garbage is walking its dogs while the street is curbing its temper, a pillow is lying in a gutter grate while a soak is saying section 8 to himself, and the decrepit front porch of an old gutted abandoned row house is being loomed over by a shadow to take in the recent decomposition of an alien opossum: the tissue-receding mandible and ribcage, the vanishing viscera, the double womb, the dental formula and the old round iron cord of the white prehensile tail lying visible just beyond the parapet. For it is portentous this opossum and I can't lament it enough: the street is a one-way street moving away from convergence towards a dead end where all the babies have babies and beards and breasts and hair between their legs and refuse to cry.

Native Son's Bigger, *Frankenstein's* fiend, on these classical creations, on these wretched visions I mull over whenever I see one of these children of spleen thrust away by foot at birth and abandoned in the shitholes of someone else's doing, for coupled with their atavistic fears one can almost see into the biological cereal bowls of their bodies, aswarm with hyperactivities and attention-deficiencies swimming inside those sugar-coated sharks, inside the hormone-induced fast foods swallowed whole, for once those monstrous mandibles and palates, embedded with the maturing seeds of molars and canines and the fissures of incisors, dribble their deciduous teeth, milk teeth, boys will grow into weed whackers and misconceived crickets—the teenage ten-year-old girls—will kill time with their legs instead of with their wings, for in the absence of surety this is what the mind does; and they'll be so warped by the torque of social quarantine that one can almost see them stuffing pretty-headed white girls into heating systems (Bigger), that or choking the shit out of them for sake of being seen by a world which otherwise wouldn't have (The Fiend). Why do you think the bus can be so terminal? Why do you think public transit excursions can be so goddamn indelible? They're loud, man, they're loud! It's as if they'll disappear if they shut up. Once I got onto this double bus and headed to the back (something I *never* do but there were empty seats), I go to the rear and sit next to this group of dark-skinned middle schoolers and I tell you no more than a minute, man, I am a hostage. They are so loud that this old Korean couple get up and go up front and they can barely walk let alone stand, but I refuse to give them that and stay where I am when the one right next to me laughs right into my ear—and then all of a sudden I can hear the decorticated peanuts in her mouth and witness the sparking bits, I can smell the smell of the bouquet of burnt hair and see the hairline bordered by bandages, yet she just keeps on munching and cursing and shit—and no one says a goddamn thing let alone the bus driver! My stop's too far away to get off early so I start rummaging around in my satchel instead, pretending I'm looking for something and elbow this little shit, not hard just enough, and she goes *damn* but I don't give a damn. She turns to one of her girlfriends then, all hush-hush-like, going *pss-pss-pss,* for that one to lean into the other two to *pss-pss-pss* and finally for the other two to *pss-pss-pss* on back, until they all go quiet-like and look at me—and then burst out laughing. Oh! they laugh and laugh, loud at first, but then the seizures ensue: the leaning-overs and the holding of the guts, the lolling of those poor burnt hot comb-abused foreheads and with those *mouths* stretching far and wide without even a flutter of a sound coming out—the noiseless laugh the loudest laugh of all! And although I'm not even looking at them everyone else is though…at them…at me (you see, last winter leave, while revisiting the Pacific, I acquired some recent mementos, scars left by the falling leaves of false beliefs, one in the corner of my mouth, one through the middle and to the side of my lower lip, one drawn across the left cheekbone and one shaped like a humongous uppercase Y on the back of my habitually shaven head, for I am freshly balding due to duress and the excessiveness of my alcohol consumption, for all the nectar I have consumed over the years, all those nights of caroling and caterwauling with the insomniacs unseen, all those tears I've sadistically shed under the maria of the moonrise have—despite partial concealment by thick prescription glasses—left little childish divots of sea water pooled beneath the toddy-titanic blowfishes of my eyes: so concerning the state of my self-esteem…needless to say is needless to say). The gut's a fist throat's dry cheeks hot, and there's this intense tingling on the tip of my throat, making it hard to swallow, but even if I could come correct what am I supposed to do, start cracking on a bunch of black girls?—Christ, that would never end! Instead I try reading *The Art Spirit*[5] and regulating my breathing, yet when we quickly take a corner I merely end up looking at this double bus bending at the joint, and then following these two fast food paper cups, anxiously repeating in goddamn quarter-circles the rhythm and pitch of the bus, and silently say to myself: stomp them. I endure their muted scorn for an infinite amount of stops, yet as soon as I alight, as soon as the doors seal behind me I distinctively hear the vulgarized maiden name of the female genitalia shouted at the back of my neck. And then another detonation of mirth. As the bus lurches. I spit on it.

I spat on her; I forget her name: a name is nothing more than a cage. She is the archetype stuck between Scylla and Charybdis, an ungodly urban ugliness and a tumultuous racial myth: black sloth. She has thick musical hair braided with many beads and her face is a button, cute as a row of them, but for such a small little bird she really has a big fucking mouth. Yet her rhymes and rhythms would really deliver though, and sometimes she would segue into this lush vulnerability of a song, for that corpulent sea creature of a schoolteacher would never fail to come alive and bark like a seal whenever she heard her—yet would always fail to answer the girl's hand: she isn't the sharpest pencil in the kit this kid, so she is called for entertainment only. This schoolteacher this washed-up slippery mass of good intention, this big old white lady who seem to sweat all the goddamn time and probably should be retired, is working way beyond her prime as a teacher, for all the years and the jaundice has made her skin as yellow as the blonde in her photograph—but what can you say? She's only a few years away, from the pension that is, and since sick women live forever, since no one's exactly falling over themselves to get to her chair, she can work as long as her yellow lungs allow.

The bird's rhyme delivery is a little too rapid and messy, yet it holds an uncomplicated savagery, for she has the six tongues of a revolver and two of the largest loudest rudest girls as endorsements. I used to check her work from time to time, but it was during the first time when I saw the bedbug coming out of her ear to listen; I used to work with a lot of children on their schoolwork to warm up on the client, patting their backs and stroking their heads (which was probably when I was marked by the omega wolf of ringworm), for when the client was too busy being lazy or in a rush (you would've swore he wrote with his toes), when he wouldn't let me help him I would help some other lamb just to get his goat—and after walking his peers through problems and paragraphs and proper pronunciations the psychology worked: after a couple of basket holds and a few of his primordial bawls in the boy's bathroom he was asking me for help. I was even able to ask about that girl, the rhymer the singer the dreamer extraordinaire, the girl whom he had stabbed in the back with her own pencil, about how he felt about it, and he told me that he didn't know how he felt about it and that he couldn't even remember doing it: *Forgotten is forgiven*,[6] Fitzgerald said. He even made a friend, before then he had none, this transfer student; at a table with the two of them, as I was making faces and building rapport, his friend said he liked me because I was a child at heart. And then he leaned into me, looking this way and that, and said that it was a good thing I was a child at heart, he was touching my thigh, because deep down down deep, he said, I'm a dirty old man.

One day the shadow is escorting the client downstairs with the third grade class, thinking he is bringing up the rear, when just beneath the second-floor landing his head is unmistakably taken for a spittoon. He looks up furiously and sees teeth, sees these three sets of gleaming white teeth cackling clear over the rail, two big and one small and with the smallest set standing on its tippy-toes, its beaded braids audible with every turn it takes towards the two bigger teeth flanking it, savoring the reaction of the once-placid animal inside a zoological garden— for they don't even have the regard to run away! Leaving the client behind the shadow climbs the mezzanine staircase, yet with each step he takes he does not grow calm cool collected as expected—on the contrary: it is only on the top stair when he realizes he is being sawed in half by butterflies. On the second-floor landing he stands before them all grinning and standing their ground, and although the shadow towers them, suspended by the tail by these tomboys, he is weak frail venomous. Surveying askance their faces he asks who did it—although he already knows who did—and finds his voice effeminized. Giggles arise. So that the shadow hawks and spits and then the two bigger teeth are laughing, the client on the mezzanine is laughing, but the shadow isn't: the bird is shivering, shoulders hunched in hot defense and with a back hand wiping a cheekbone. She stands there. They all just stand there. Until the shadow turns heads downstairs and retrieves his client before passing beneath the second-floor landing.

MARE FECUNDITATIS

BODIES, houses of scars, the places we have been: one day, dear heart, as your mother had been, rather than on the other side of this drawing you are going to be on the other side of a cleansing, cast down by stroke or fall or diabetic coma and left helpless in the hell of my heart; it could happen tomorrow today or next year—twenty centuries from now when you are *vexed to nightmare by a rocking cradle,*[7] and what rough beast would you find at the foot of your bed, waiting to give you your due, waiting with two plastic basins of water, one being solely water while the other would have in it a sudarium soon to be sainted by blood lymph and thumbprint and the mark of some tallow soap, formed from the suet of a slaughterhouse. An acid bath. I would have a look like an ax and an unthinkable act already marshaling motives in the back of my mind, harboring a heart, and an angst wrenching away at the bones—and I will feel you I will ache you I will cry you, for when the falling leaf of a false belief is as crushing as an eyelash against the cheek, when your lips are closest to mine, asking for that final favor that release, I can't say what I would do: my conscience is a sentence.

Ghettoes and slums are not the same: if everyone is ethnically alike they are ghettoes, if everyone is just basically poor they are slums; we are a ghetto in a slum, you and I, the Facility suits us, for these low-cost duplexes newly constructed of cardboard and kiddy glue is just another fenced-in slum with its false hopes and doors and walls so thin that you could hammer a nail through the cranium-buttressed wall of the apoplectic next door. Our duplex has one ground-floor apartment where a veteran invalid and his offspring reside and one upstairs apartment where we are, and since you cannot take steps everyday you sometimes plop your packaged mass down onto the bottom step and bracing yourself on the stair and banister above scoot and heave yourself up, whereas upon descending this system is reversed by bracing yourself on the stair and banister below, all the while breathing as though through a straw; it is not only an extraordinary physcial feat but a mental one as well, for after a two years of this, by the haul and dragging of your enormity, the center lips of these wooden steps have adopted the polished appearance of mahogany, for only upstairs apartments were available at the time of your move and since then no one in a downstairs apartment has ever had the pleasure of moving or passing away. Despite my forewarning from out west you rented it, because the third sister was only a half a block away and because of the low-cost living, only to find yourself sliding down or crawling up the steps like a bitch with a broken back, because despite accommodating advances, unless you are a complete cripple, Medicare doesn't care for a chairlift. There are six duplexes in a row and six more across a dividing walk, twelve in a section with three sections altogether and we are either black or brown or red inside of this fenced-in slum, inside of these side-by-side shoeboxes double-stacked that you can't help forever feeling like the recently procured pet respiring through pencil-punched-out holes, not to mention the outer claustrophobia of the ghetto encroaching you.

After returning home I had first acquired an apartment in the Italian Market, but had to forfeit it for sake of the Academy and materials. I had refused the bedroom (your request) which of course has a door (you felt it more important for me to have a door), The room's darker, you said, you can think; however my studio and living quarters became the fourteen-foot-square living room and the bed became the cot mattress on the carpet, But you an illustrator, you said, after learning of my acceptance letter, and then started in on how drawing some makeshift curtain closed to keep me separate from the kitchen stove light wouldn't work…and you were right: to illustrate means *to bring to light*. But how can you go into dark places if you don't have a goddamn door to close? So two portmanteaus two portfolios two easels and two boxes of literature were shifted from the living room to the ten-foot-square bedroom (a portion of the initial fourteen-foot square having been allotted to a water heater and a closet), a room with two opposing doors, one leading to the small kitchen and bathroom compressed by these two rooms and the other down to a little tiny brown eye patch of grass (which never sees any light), and your possessions, the battleship of your bed, your prehistoric television, the sturdiness of your dresser (fucking oak: invalids have the heaviest furniture), and that terrible transferable toilet (its mood alone weighting more than it's worth), were jostled and slid and carried off towards that living room like the lumbaginous invalids that they are, which alongside that brass elephant nightstand, that reclining wooly mammoth of a chair, and that sizable shrine (a roomy broken-down lopsided speaker-supported glassless entertainment cabinet void of an entertainment system, a boxed amalgam peopled with a polychromatic explosion of miniature stuffed animals, embroidered imaginary beasts, pachydermatous trinkets and figurines [your obsession with the gentle giant], a plastic spider plant, fragrantly decayed roses, gilded genealogical limbs inside of variously sized picture frames, a long forgotten musical jewel box [tinny with its tiny Brailled engine], a terrible big black leather-bound Bible with cherry-forked tongue lolling from pages trimmed with gold, a Wolof ebony mask inlayed with bone, a half-carven half-crazed ebonized leopard in midleap jutting from the hunk of baobab I brought back from Dakar [from the upside-down devil tree of Dakar], the birthday mother's day get-well thank-you cards all scarred with scribble and scrawl, as well as other bric-a-brac beggaring description) bullied much of the space, leaving only the jagged crooked path.

So that now, in the bedroom, I am watching your gestural flow from behind a field easel, that rhythm of motion that stillness of life, for I am moving from behind the borders of your body for the nude drawing you will sit for six straight days for...and on the seventh we will rest. Yet during these days I will give you plenty of breaks and back massages and will often place into the palm of your hand, like alms, Percocet upon Percocet at ten milligrams each, seven tablets a day, or simply give the eighty milligrams of Oxycontin, the green pill, and then watch you slide down that rabbit hole. For I will memorize you. Like slaughtered ox meat I will see every piece of you hooked and splayed on the back of my lids. Yet before we started, while fitting this large drawing board upon the field easel, you hobbled in, wheezing and wearing a slightly knee-back-pained look on the face and a holey nightgown, the right tit hanging half-out, brown, half-covered with yellow lace as if a giant imperial moth had emerged: you would do anything for your sons and for an artist this shamelessness is an asset, yet for a son it's an excruciation. I wouldn't be so shameless with a body like yours, I wouldn't be so brazen with a halo of pain, for once the nightgown was unraveled I found you sitting in front of me as naked as the day you were dawned, but in such a different way that I couldn't stand the sight of you: it was like staring into a solar eclipse, a phenomenon not meant to be seen by the naked eye. It is nothing like the times when I would catch you hobbling about the apartment nude or upon the pliable throne, this time you are naked not nude, exposed in bone and soul, this time your state of undress is intentional rather than accidental, sedentary instead of momentary. Even so: during these series of croquis, while hearing what your fig-ureless form has to say, the fear grows thinner and thinner and bit-by-bit your body begins to imbue my own. I will begin to receive, I believe, a slow sense of instruction.

How to scale and envelop the body, how to pull away from fractions, to treat the whole as a whole as an organic thing, to triangulate to modulate to shape parts in relation to one another, to achieve general proportion before solidifying to move in and chisel away with meticulousness: all of this and more was instilled in me within the Academy, for this fervent professor would hammer and harangue me incessantly, this archaic German who was impatient as hell only because most of his *patients* were impatient as hell, a hospital of horrible draftsmen, and say that I should first find the gestural flow, that all forms possess it, that rhythm of motion that stillness in life; draw vigorously he would say, but with acuity and care and when the time comes to hone in, tonally, the parts should progress together. Yet before the body there were first the still lifes: the arabesque-embroidered draperies and costumes, the period-piece golems and the infertile flowers, the seal-like bowling shoes and the prurient classic cola bottles along side the lackluster pots spoons swords fruits door knobs, you know, random shit, and then we moved from the newly wrought studio building to the historic museum and cast hall: busts statues friezes reliefs, Greek and Roman duplicates as well as a *David*, Michelangelo's Goliath standing over twenty feet tall with his stony cream curls touching the ceiling almost and yet with that greatly disproportionate elfin phallus banished between the groined vault of his lower limbs. Lastly we sallied forth to meet the human being and we would be up there just hatching and cross-hatching away at the tones with our growing understanding of musculature and skeletal schema, scaffolding our intentions while feeling this slight hair-thin surge in our guts, as if we were in receipt of something greater than ourselves—and yet we of it—with the tips of our drawing implements possessing nerve endings which leapt to life upon touching the virtual form. Still we had to step back and look for harmony as a whole, you can draw a really great face,

my rival would say, an exceptional draftsmen and a Mescalero
Apache who had moved all the way from the desert wilderness
of the Southern West to slave inside a suburban supermarket
inside the Northern East, you can draw a really great face,
he would hypothetically declare, but the whole body could be
falling apart—and that's exactly it, because your whole body
is falling apart, except for your face: for with the teeth put in
and the chin put up, despite the dimpled forehead, your face
tomorrow will be as free from furrow as it is today. Yet before
the Academy I just eyed it, for in spite of astigmatism and
awful eyesight with optical aids I have a pretty good eye. In
intuition I trust. I listen to the figure to the moods to how it
wants to be drawn, for the Academy may have taught me the
technical side, how to shape things out, but I taught myself
how to look…without looking away.

Following our quotidian studies the rival and *the rat* would
go about like two escorts preparing for potential conquests,
models who were sometimes nude or not, sometimes women
or men, sometimes our colleagues or us: we posed for each
other, clothed and unclothed. And since all the cast rooms
have large curtain-less windows we would wait for the sun to
set to use our own light source, although due to the studio
building blocking the windows we would only really receive
indirect light. We'd rearrange the chairs easels stools and the
small portable stage, we'd remove from the closet the blanket the pillow and the heater or the fan, lay out props and
put up backdrops if props and backdrops were needed, and
make sure that the timer was ready to measure the length of
the poses and the breaks, so that once the model was in place
we would reposition the heater or the fan, making sure the
model was warm not hot, cool not cold, and in homage to

Caravaggio and his tenebrists we would readjust the overhead lamp that was tall and bent in the shape of a crane, so that that single beam of light could be concentrated on the actor on the stage. Imbued by this theatric once we marshaled several models in chiaroscuro for a terrible tableau vivant which found us lightheartedly yelling *pose* as if saying *quiet* to everyone near, mocking those automatons at Illuminati, this classic atelier founded by a narcissistic *monomyth* of the bourgeois art clinic. But the best appearances of the models were actually when they were just getting ready or just resting on stage, yet even if a pose wasn't necessarily arresting we would fight the temptation to touch it and walk around it instead, crouching and squinting, hunting for a better angle. Angle is everything. If you move just a few inches to your right, the rival would say, you would have a completely different drawing, and so we would walk around it, parallactically moving it shifting it stalking it as the sketch hunter optimizing his hunt, and once assured of such we would set up our easels, splay out our supplies, sit or stay standing to take in another good look, imagining the figure on the paper before even lifting a finger. If we were executing mass drawings we would've already smeared a base coat of charcoal sticks and shavings over entire sheets of white paper until we had instituted a medium-gray ground, then we would steadying our sticks, squint at our studies, open our eyes and attack.

Squinting is god. It negates detail and yet proposes it. It reduces everything to simple geometric shapes, the building blocks of a good drawing, revealing only the foundation the very thing that makes a thing what it is. After scaffolding a figure outline on gray ground you can block and wipe out all the dark darks with the broadside of a charcoal stick and all the white whites with a soft chamois and a kneaded eraser, and even at this stage if the shape sizes are correct and rightly placed the drawing, albeit abstract, should be looking like the model already; and throughout the drawing's crescendo squinting eyes should be opening up often so that the values can be orchestrated across the flesh, yet keeping the tone masses in concert, breaking them up only when necessary like for a hightlighted protuberance or a drapery wrinkle. Yet you have to be careful because if you don't take the time to step back and just look you'll destroy it—and then damn, the German will say to you, considering your work, that was a pretty good drawing, goddamn, before you started to doodle over it. But it was an Academy pioneer, one of The Eight,[8] a man who had had the insight of a lightning bolt, having said that *one who knows what is under the skin will understand the slightest change on the surface, he sees the slightest sign that has meaning and is not deceived by accidents,*[9] who had really inspired the drawing of your body, and in turn I would receive, I believe, a slow sense of instruction: the maternal nude must not be amassed, it must not be measured by a plumb line or a spin top attached to a fishing wire; you must not make a light envelope of the body, for proportion will be pointless. Want something essential. Tradition stifles. Care less whether you have accord or not, trust the mind to make patterns. Instead of toning out the body parts together hone in on one member at a time and then draw another one under that different angle of light, under that different angle of looking, for the nude the mirror will surely show the shatters of your inner depths. Stop before perfection. Walk away. For although most realists—imaginary beings obsessed with literalisms for lack of imagination—will commonly agree that the drawing has turned out to be an incongruous mess...

you should continue this approach. It's quite haphazard but it can surface some interesting results, some intersecting symbols. Imagination manhandles memory, transfigures for the desired effect which can turn out rather ruthless or tender or a tad bit grotesque—but isn't what we're looking at what we're looking with? You should never sacrifice beauty to make it ugly or ugliness to make it pretty. Mistakes will be made: disproportionate parts mismatched features unsutured tones, despite stepping back, but a mistake can prove to be the effective thing. Beauty is an accident of birth. And an advantageous accident can prove to be the duende of the drawing, the owner of the house. Or not. Understand: have no compunctions about killing your babies, but not before they are babies. For when they are still tasting that sweet temptation to exist, who knows if they will fail to fulfill the labor.

On the first day croquis are created, hard and soft carbonized twigs of willow and vine are employed, manipulating them this way and that, broadside even on large sheets of finely toothed cream paper and it is symbolic: I am washing the body, I am caressing it with eyes ash and imagination instead of with hands soap and water, for on the second day now the time has come to see, come and see the body seems to say to me, and so I switch to graphite and a smooth white drawing sheet, for throughout the course of four more days various gradient graphite tones will be exploited to push the drawing progressively darker, an extremely meticulous biopsy that will take a total of sixteen hours to complete, for although your scars will not be depicted per se, except for the ones on the forehead and the stomach, they will be far from immaterial. For I will fall. Floating from body part to body part in no particular order. And in this way throughout its stages the drawing will take on the look of a mythological god with bits and pieces of body being realized at random, for the nude as off-putting as it seems will spring to life, will blush and gush with vitality.

———————

IT IS A GRUESOME MAP OF TRIUMPH, visas of cicatrices bearing witness to the terra incognita of unsightly turns and dips, indecently sited creases, gargantuan curves and a grotesque gouge that are both topography and testimony to me: you are one big human surgery, a map of the soul. For my love, I am drawing your face, and while fleshing out the indentation of your forehead the procedure recurs: it is evidence this fissure in thought of the tumor whose rumor would've wrought paralysis on the right side of your body, whose removal resulted in an antibiotic-defiant bug contracted in intensive care, holding you hospital-ridden for two additional weeks; out I fish the stories of those great trout eyes those once-upon-a-time cataracts those milky clouds caught in absent skies and the right retina's burst blood vessel due to the devils of diabetes; the whole face and skull is sculpted as is the Adam's apple the goiter, hung askew and oppositely of the surgical seam where the twin apple had been, as though you were two men in one woman, having leaned and drew away from these solicitous treatments to make sure you were looking like you. No: to make sure you were looking more you than you do yourself. Water? Yes. But I don't give gospel. I give opiates. I can't study with song, for the earplugs are to plug me in: the respirations of one's ocean are symphonic, and the basest whisper from the lips can be as explicit as the smallest suspension in a chamber of the heart.

Standing you would be preferable, just long enough for me to feel the anguish of your lower back the seat of your

misery and the ungainly walk and weight crushing down on
those knobby little knees of yours, your lower legs being the
only skinniness on you, making mine tingle with a twitch. If I
ask you would stand but I don't carry that strand of cruelty—
yet the small of the back that's where it's at, that's where it was,
L5-S1, that slipped disk for you had slipped and fell at the post
office over twenty-five years ago and whose monthly compen-
sations has been our source of income ever since. Now tormented by acute spinal pinches losing weight might help, but
the wrong diet might send you down that diabetic shock corri-
dor, for you nodded off once transporting your obese niece, for
your blood sugar had plummeted and consciousness was lost
at the wheel and although the curb caught the car what was
preventing *you* from catching anywhere from forty winks to infinity?—and since the niece couldn't drive a car, since she's list-
less, she didn't call an ambulance or even turn off the engine;
she just sat there listening to the radio, figuring you were just
tired: you were cocooning into a coma. But half an hour later
by the pity of god and being illegally parked you were awo-
ken—and it was just that, pity, for you were just about to mount
the Schulykill Expressway. So since I can't study you standing
I can't capture the psychosis of your knee either, that right
kneecap replacement that moon-faced madwoman forged of
dementia's ore and forever to go off in downpour and madden
metal detectors, I could lie you down on the floor and stand
over you, but that would be over the top; besides I found you
on the floor before, floating on your back in a puddle of piss
inside a dilapidated row house, for I was staying with you by
chance after having departed a city with another city in sight
and despite rubber tub and fluffy floor mats, handlebars and
pleas, you slipped from the tub and couldn't get up and when

I came to the door four or five hours later (you always leave the door open, so you can listen to your music) you were lying naked on the tiles with your eyelids closed and your chest not moving—and I almost went mad. I dropped to my knees and shook you. You were asleep—not *asleep* asleep, just asleep. Said since no one could hear you, since no one could get in through the bars on the windows and the doors, you'd just went on to sleep and hoped that you would have the strength to get up when you woke up, and I got mad. I put you back into the tub, I washed off your water, I helped you out and clothed you, all the while listening to the deafening silence of your record player speakers, for the needle had long returned to the cradle and was playing nothing at all for the foreseeable future.

Drawing the torso will be tortuous so I sally forth to meet the other parts of your body: the first scars I could ever remember you having are on the upper parts of your arms, for on the left arm there is the circular tuberculosis inoculation, a regulation that had been discontinued the year I was born the year of the rat, and on the right there is an archipelago of keloids, more prominent scars predating me like tribal scarifications, leavened by the glass particles that were showered into your flesh: you were heavy with the second son then, with the firstborn in the backseat being a two-year-old and the father driving and the body was young and shapely then, skinny but not skinny and the father had less of that killjoy quality in him, for it wasn't his fault, the accident, and with the exception of you everyone born and not-yet-born had walked away scot-free. And look, near the clavicle: stabbed by the fifth sister's mistress, for you were trying to get your nephew away from that house, for after having been lassoed in utero by narcotics he was still living with his mother as a baby in his mid-twenties then, but he had first called your mother his grandmother and subsequently your third sister was supposed to pick him up, because your mother couldn't drive, but then the third sister couldn't pick him up because she was probably picking up one of *her* five grandchildren and so *you* had to pick him up—and *he* had to pick off his mother's mistress with a good swift kick in the kidney before she could puncture any of your vitals. Or maybe he grabbed her? I think he grabbed her, because that would explain the scar on the back of his hand and that severed nerve. For my love, I am drawing your hands, the fingers and the bunched-up joint skin, the horny ivory-pinks, for I am seeing the sluggish treks they tend to take cross telephone tomes: your hands look like elephants, my hands look like elephants, yet despite the simile we share we look nothing alike: the first-born looks more like you than I, a squat bronze body with a sturdy back, while I look more like the father and the second son, tall and broad-shouldered and pitch-night in certain light. And look there, trailing down the inside of your wrist: the vertical incision that was made to avoid the obvious, a long stitching from that compressed-nerve-alleviating procedure, for you had developed carpal tunnel from typing at the post office which in turn was aggravated by the fall. You are forever falling: you fell for the father you fell for the office you fell for the tub, you even fell for a cardboard box stuffed with yesterday's newspaper, a waterlogged *Inquirer* swaddled in plastic wrap to give the box the illusive heaviness of a videocassette recorder; you are forever falling for something or falling apart or just plain falling. In any case after accomplishing the hands I skip down to sculpt those tiny edematous feet—pitifully tortured things—and even wrestle with the chubby loincloth of fat, hiding pudendum and dusty menopause alike, yet I can no longer duck the torso.

The *Mansion of Horus:* you have the six breasts of a bovine being with two huge flaccid breasts with a solar disk in between and a meaty midriff divided down the middle by a scar, which is nothing more than two sizable stacks of flesh with a stack-crease on either flank, giving them the appearance of two additional bosoms, minus the lowest left breast the sixth: a Hathor with an indentation instead of a tit. And yet those flanks look like two asses to me too, lying sideways and facing out, with the lowest left cheek being bitten out, a chunk the size of a grapefruit. For that hole came from carelessness, from you constantly setting down an uncapped insulin needle and then injecting yourself with it, over and over in the same spot, yet you were supposed to rotate the spots, you were supposed to shoot up in the fatty part of your arms or in the outer reaches of your thighs, the stomach, to rotate them so that the flesh won't gangrene in any given place; and since the doctor was afraid to stitch you (you being so big and—due to diabetes steroids and depression—gaining still) you were left open to heal from inside out, so when your mother would come over to wash you that whole hand would be inside your hole and it drove you wild. Yet what is torturous to you is unimaginable to me, so whenever you're complaining about the mundane pettiness of the planets, about the minor apocalypses, I remember what your first sister told me to do whenever the pain's talking over you: Take what she says, son, and cut it in half.

Five stomach surgeries. Sounds like a German play. Four from complications and one from a joke you've forgotten. The chief incisions, however, the ones that would set the tone to avoid any unnecessary scarring in the future, the guidelines sort of speak for three successive surgeries, were sliced in the shape of the singular letter I. That I came from a partial hysterectomy; I remember it vividly. Hysteria comes from hysterectomy, way back when a woman's womb was removed it was believed she would go insane and act hysterical, so I guess this was what happened to you. I was seven. Maybe not. I tend to plug everything into that age. One of your ovaries had dislocated and was rotting inside and so it had to be removed along with the womb, yet days later in my room, the second son's and mine, kneeling bedside as if praying to rather than playing with a four-inch-tall action figure, I had heard your laughter coming down the hall; the second son was taking apart some appliance to put it back together while I was manipulating my men, involved in some private scene (our scenes, the second son's and mine, were grand adventures), when we heard the darkest laugh of our lives. Only yesterday we had bullied you with pushy questions, asking if it hurt asking if it itched asking if we could see it—we were obsessed with seeing it: the scalpel had roughly gone across to where the two stack-creases would meet, about three inches in length, picked up at the center of this incision to slice down the middle for six inches (removing your very first and dearest scar: forever unbellybuttoned), and then picked up again to finish with the final cut, parallel and equal to the first, bordering the pubis—for it would serve as a double door for sake of successive surgeries. It was a sight. A sight to behold. But then there were the other sights too, for when I would ask about the body the eyes would ask for more: O, so you want to see what they feel like today? Yet you would never say this to make me feel embarrassed or amiss—matter of fact, though I often second-guess it, my deadliest memory is one of your breasts, for you were washing from the bathroom basin when I had toddled in and pointed at it and you said that I used to suck it, that I was the only one who had, and when I shook my head you took it and aimed it at my eyes and even after my flight into bed, even after the wailing, the shadow of your laugh would come running down the hall.

The father did it. The father made you laugh. You don't even remember the joke. All you remember is that the two of you were in bed and that you couldn't stop laughing: you laughed so hard you burst your stitches. Laughter curdled to gurgle. Blood steeped the bedspread. And as you were looking down at yourself sneaking out like a bloody audience, shifting with the promise of more to come, you went quite mad and started to moan—for although the I was sewn with stitches resembling ridges and fastened with four thick tubular staples encased in plastic, like the laces of a tight-fitting corset, they popped and flew open anyoleway and so when we hear the noise, the blood noise and the moans, all three of your sons come running out of their rooms and into yours where we are blinded by the domestic attire of our father, wearing a white V-neck T-shirt...and nothing else; he is kneeling over you— you who are folded like a fetus beside a backgammon brief-case opened to a game—and the first glimpse from behind the brothers is of the crack of the father's ass and his dark tumescent testicles and of his hands trying and prying your arms free so that he can see, so that we all can see...when he shifts: the seat of your grit, the tenderness and the pity peek-ing out in the glistening and coming blood—and the smell, my god, the smell: I swear on my eyes I can see the smell cooking, the fishy fumes the steam rising the hot tentacled air—and I can the taste the tang of iron in it too; so that my stomach is churning and the father is telling the second son to get the lastborn out, get him out get him out, and he is pushing me and pushing me and keeps on pushing me until we are down the hall and in our room; the firstborn stays. Moments later two white paramedics come bounding up the stairs behind the firstborn with their collapsible stretcher handbags and stethoscopes, and once in your room they disappear behind the door after he closes it. And I don't know why but I'm not afraid, not at all, just embarrassed and anxious—not for what is happening to you but what is happening to those men: I hate having sleepovers because I never know whether the father's going to wear underwear or not. I can see you wearing underwear and nothing else, but a *T-shirt* and nothing else…that just throws me off. I am embarrassed and sorry for those white paramedics, for they're in there right now working over your gushing belly under his bloodshed undershirt, looking like Winnie the Pooh, and yet it isn't long before I'm seeing him fully dressed and opening the door, holding handbags while guiding the paramedics out who're carrying you out on that stretcher in your gauzy layers of alizarin crimson, and as they're maneuvering you through the hall and down the steps and out the door the second son and the lastborn are crouching at the top step, catching the firstborn bringing up the rear, just before he's stepping down into the sunshine. Yet when the father and him reappear in the vestibule he is nodding like an idiot, and he is still struggling with the instructions after the father leaves us alone. We risk the room then to see the bloodbath on your side of the bed, and I can't remember how old I was but I remember the pattern on the bedspread: it was an orange mountain range that had repeated itself incessantly and where the belly had bled there was a huge red sun setting inside a valley. We were watching this sun until we retired to our rooms. I started playing again. The second son was watching. I started making combat noises and when he couldn't take it anymore he just spat at me. It was getting late. What we are going do? I asked. What are you going to eat? I'm starving.

They kept irrigating your innards with saline solution until they got you to the hospital; more surgery was required. Turns out, you will relay years later, the father never stayed with you, not that night or any other and I have to wonder: where was he calling from when he called home? Was it really from the hospital or from the other woman's apartment? Regardless the wound had trouble healing and six months after that another egg was found rotting inside, so they reopened the I. Your father was the first to notice it, you said, could smell it coming from my cootie cat—as if I was dying to know. Smelled terrible, you said, smelled the way catfish smell wrapped inside cheap plastic wrap and left inside a broken-down refrigerator to rot. And I told you thank you. Thank you very much. Yet even after the doctor told you what it was, even after he told you to refrain from fucking before and after surgery, you did it anyway, before *and* after, because *he* wanted to: That's just one of the things you do, you said, when you married; always fulfill your female duties. Even used to wash your daddy. Now that's love. But then you were reopened for a third time, this time for scar removal, for the scars were fairly wrapping themselves around your organs, choking them, causing the bleeding from within.

Dear heart, your stomach has been opened five times: four times by surgical steel and once from a joke you've forgotten— which probably wasn't even that funny. Although the father, forever the infectious, with that indomitable sense of humor of his, has this charismatic way of making you want to believe that it was. Funny: will I ever show you the drawing? No. I won't even want to look at it myself. It will be one of the finest works I've ever orchestrated: *Movement No. 12 (the Artist's Mother)*.

An exhibition will want show it but won't, another will want to honor it and will, yet when a loaded crone will want to pay me handsomely for it I will tell her thank you, no, I'm paying for it myself, and then stash it underneath an unknown opening in the closet. It will be ruined a couple of weeks afterwards. By water damage and mold.

MARE NECTARIS

THE PARTHENON, the Museum of Art, the arms and armor wing is overrun this first Friday morn of May, the day of an exhibition, inside this medieval mythology I am being besieged by a legion of little ones running amok amidst the solemn majesty of the ancient, the world-conquering weaponry of European moaks, the masters of all knowledge: the would-be-patina-ridden rondaches and aegises of fifteen-century Italy, French cuirassiers and German gauntlets and burgonets, sundry broad swords halberds and boar spears, needle-like rapiers and war scythes, the gilded flintlock pistol prize and on top of these the preserved nerve lies; yes yes, their loutish laughter knows solely fire no fear no helmet, yet to the

memorial beauty of silent study sound is worse than any sol-
vent, clamor more coercive than any agent, disharmony more
despoiling than any steaming bag of shit, for their tongues,
dedicated to Mars, has slashed canvases unprepared for such
cacophony downstairs in the European paintings department
and are now upstairs jabbering and hammering away at the
centuries of truce long last won from time and rust by a dedicated detail of conservators under the curatorial commands
of adamant madams and men. During the Academy days
the rival had confided in me inside the European paintings
department that he felt sadly amazed at how bored he is of
this museum, that it does not marry much in him, that he
came all the way from the desert wilderness to be left high
and dry with Gauguin, that what little art the museum has
he had in less than two years exhausted everything: in various compositions, in multiple charcoal and graphite drawings
(for ink isn't allowed in this sanctum sanctorum), he sketched
out all the prominent master sculptures on display (Degas's
Ballerina and Rodin's *Mother and Child* and *Woman Taken Unawares* to name a few), he rendered numerous bas-reliefs such
as the Seasons (Flora Ceres Bacchus Saturn), he executed
small-scale grisailles (for anything bigger than fourteen-by-
seventeen isn't allowed either) and isolated color studies of
the worthwhile master paintings in oil to lastly conduct pains-
taking studies of much of the archival drawings, so that in
the two years he had been in my city he felt that he had sadly
and aptly exhausted this *tomb*. How can you exhaust Eakins's
most momentous folly, his magnum opus *The Agnew Clinic*, the
viewing of a live surgery through the treasure-sunken eyes of
an all-male medical audience fixed upon a woman's deathly
pale bosom, her incision peeled back by jeweler's forceps like

labia in bloom? How can you condemn Tanner's *The Annunciation*, that biblical vision of blinding-white spermatozoa pulsating through the crack of the curtained door, the lines of the shelf bed carpet all angling towards it as is the idyllic expression of our reticent Mary, swaddled in drapery folds and blanket resembling the beach-dried tentacles of a school of squids? What of the soft indelible whorls of the *Water Mill* by Thaulow or *The Print Collector* and *The Imaginary Illness*, the unfussy drollery of Daumier's wit? What of Picasso's *Chrysanthemums* and that slightly grotesque *Head of a Woman* (Parisian lady of the night), or the sanatorium window view of Van Gogh's *Rain?*—the music makes you want to take your clothes off again! How can you dismiss Whistler's mostly monochromic *Nocturne*—the groan of a foghorn can be heard throughout that dark ominous bay—or the cutthroat aristocracy of *The Moorish Chief* (*The Harem Guard*), which would bemuse you as to how Charlemont, an Austrian, could capture with such keen ferocity the northern African's self-possession? Dalí's *Soft Construction with Boiled Beans (Premonition of Civil War)*—an orgy of body parts and maggoty beans crawling under a lake of clouds breached by cerulean and with that fragment of firmament framed by the acute monstrosity of a right angle, a wicked number seven, a dramatically bent leg attached to a human head and foot and a nipple-ripe mango gripped by a bifurcated finger—can never be deleted. Dalí described this painting as *a vast human body breaking out into monstrous excrescences of arms and legs tearing at one another in a delirium of auto-strangulation.*[10] What bullshit! What a pretentious piece of crap. But I love it! Yet the rival feels that his unbridled ambition has exhausted his eyes indubitably, leaving him dreadfully bored to tears. A tomb? A tomb! I should cut out his tongue.

A student of strategy of precision, carefully I scope out the artifacts and the point of entry then set up the foldout stool, yet it isn't exciting so I move to another spot, sit and look then reach into the satchel for the implements: a folder is always stocked with charcoal sheets ranging in texture and temperature and of course there are always the earplugs, for in this wing of arms and armor there is a massive amount of mouths running amok, their *ooos* and *ahhhs*, their look-at-this and look-at-thats, their weirds and their pretties and their little bum ditties—I mean they never shut up: children should be seen not heard. Yet on gray paper on a clipboard, in charcoal and white chalk, for hours I have been shaping the blackened back of French cuirassier armor that had been fashioned for a corpulent man, and even with the skull thrust with fluorescent earplugs these sunny barbarians can't even *see* that I can hear them. Most of them are oblivious but some are chivalrous: they know at least to shut the hell up when over me; like with these Korean twins here, these porcelain dolls, I heard them coming through the earplugs, yet instead of growing louder as they drew nearer their voices grew softer, so that now I don't even think that they're children: they're as quiet as houseplants. Presently a black white-headed girl with bone ash skin frosted eyelashes and eyes the color of slapped cheeks, cheeks the buttocks of cherries and a lugubrious lower lip, an albino, is behind me, just as that beggar had been behind me at the airport, that odd archetype of Dakar. We had traded smiles before I returned to the cuirass and she has been standing behind me now for a good twenty minutes or so, saying not a word moving not a muscle. She must be around eleven. Her body is coming alive very early. It narcotizes the air. Pressed against the nape of my neck her condensed scent burgeons the bird-of-paradise, the warrior flower the distended clitoris the bird which distracts with the plumage of a spear, for my drunken inamorata had painted it as such: with loud candy colors, florescent oranges and yellows and reds, Medusa Marie, a *tragic mulatta* in myth, had expressed herself on my shaft after I had expressed that I too could be a partaker of both flesh, woman's and man's, for at thirty-two I had found myself being opened up by that godlike woman-child, who at thirty-four would go on to teach me much in matters of love. From time to time as she painted she would spit on her fingertips to graze the teats of my black breasts—memories of my androgyny—to maintain that extravagant fulfillment of blood between brush strokes until she put me out of my misery by climbing onto the colors: Libido is the desire to learn, my love—so that now there is this intensity this solitude this schism of the heart whenever I am riven by her recording: *I called you. You had called and left a long and rambling message and I was not sure. Surprisingly you answered: you live by close and want to come. On purpose I dress down; let him see me let me be seen. I have my period; it is the beginning or the middle. It is damp outside, rained, and I am putting on my favorite parts: music and pants, huge loose black cotton worn like an old T-shirt with frayed bottoms. The street is dark wet, many not around, a quiet road, a one way road when I meet you outside and did I smoke?, always embarrassing, and saw you from afar. I remember you were familiar to me: an easy hello, a smart man a handsome man a man who still practices the dying art of dialogue. We become late-arrivals.* Perception is enough. For I am receiving this godlike woman-child with such volatile clarity that I squirm on my stool: other than for a February millenary night with an Arab Jew (which merely aggravated Eros) I haven't pulled myself out of a woman in well over a year and I am becoming more and more distrait because of Andromaque's lay (yet she is another story). Excuse me. Ah! she trawls a toe to test the water, and for the girl I unplug an ear. Excuse me, echoes through the birdlike halls of her bones, I don't mean to bother you (you) but if you don't mind me saying (saying)…and then doesn't. *Rebecca's (eleven p.m.?): we walk in briskly, let ourselves in, I do knowing they are out back and my brother among them around the Thanksgiving bonfire and two rooms in we meet Rebecca's normally placid bitch; you walk up not considering, saying something you feel she may understand and then hold out your hand, so that she can smell your allegiance and your recent adventures.* Go on, I say, say what you have to say, noting the pinches of powdered sugar on her puberulent forearms, and she says, You might want to step away from your drawing. *She bites! A big bloody. And from the palm of your hand a chunk of you is sticking out like a deathly white tongue, quickly lapped up by a syrup of blood. Your whole hand is consumed and you hold it up to keep the blood in, asking for a bathroom when Rebecca and Sand come in—with that normally placid bitch just trotting away.* I try keeping her around, I try keeping her at bay: I would never touch you that way, I want to say, for the girl bears the mother through the woman. Yet the girl just slips away, leaving behind her phantom in the warlike hairs of my nostrils. Dedicated to Mars. *You are calm and collected. You are murderous. Strange angle to your jaw, tension at the root of your neck and the downward pull of that crouched animal in the corner of your lips, that laugh line I will link to liquor. Were you drinking before we met, even then?* Merely minutes pass before I can't even be in this room this place this tomb! I can't go back to this, I'm thinking, nor can I go on at the Academy. *I don't know what to do, stand behind you in the bathroom feeling useless? Wondering if we'll be spending the night at Highland. You blot you blot you blot, but it is a loss; a little more conviction and she would've had a finger. You blot some more sterilize then gauze. Two Alabama white girls, lovers, stand unspeaking the unspoken obvious truth: all night strange that Rebecca's normally placid bitch would bite you. My brother in the back as well, quiet and withdrawn after being bit four times by others, walks the other way when this one comes around…and yet you held out your hand. Ah!: all night the all-too obvious.* I'm better than them, I'm thinking, the Apache is my only rival. Some people don't have the gift, I understand that—but they don't even have the *gift certificate* and I'm posing for them! What about the firstborn? I ask myself. You can always swallow that bulbous vacuous mass you call pride and ask for a co-sign on a loan. Pride? Pride! What the *fuck* is pride? *The night passed away and Rebecca kept offering you more and more whiskey and precautions. You probably shouldn't be drinking, you said, if you want the bleeding to stop; you don't have the coverage. It's like experiencing Thanksgiving in reverse, I said, and then you did what is so honorable and true: you smiled despite the consequences. Just how you will make me smile, laugh even even in sleep—and when I awake you'll just smile and say what was so funny and I won't even know. You said I had asked if you wanted me to spend the night as comfort, but this I fail to remember; in the car it is you who ask if you could spend the night. And I say yes. But no sex.* Excuse me, says a suit, breaking the double helix of thought, I didn't want to bother you before but how long have you been drawing that armor? He is the curator of this department, the person who oversees the conservations of this reliquary of war—and I am enthused by the prospects of a commission, of my work hanging in his office or of some prestigious crone hiring me on as a pet project. Do you know your armor?…that's a shame, he says, it gets pretty lonely not having someone to talk to about the conservation of armor. So after some protest on the man's part I give him the drawing gratis, and while I'm departing the Parthenon, while I'm descending its celebrated stairs a zephyr of déjà vu ripples through mnemonic tissue and I am remembering these steps at this very moment, for that woman up there, the one who just grazed me, had done so in my dream...yet as soon as it comes it goes: how many times, I am wondering, have I missed passing myself on the street for sake of a set route? *You are find-ing my arms hard to find. The blood temperature climbs and the chemistry holds a treachery: you need to vomit. It subsides though and your eyes roll back into place. I hold you, the aroma of the soft lamb's wool of your armpits drives me closest, but then you slide down to pin me with the tip of your tongue and for the ankles to hum and for the sex to exile the asth-ma—for I am happening with you I am happening you! I graze your nipple and mount you to reach behind myself to insert a digit, taking your temperature (all your life, you will say to me, you had a slight temperature), and when we transpose my hands are holding your over-stuffed back with those terrible lashes switched in like crisscrossed centipedes having burned themselves together into atomic shadows...but then I am holding you to-gether again like a wet grocery bag. I raise my lips to your whiskey-filled eyes only for us to transpose once more and for me to squat again. Thana-tos is freezing his ass off outside in the rain, wearing sneakers and now and again squeaking obscenities on the kitchen tiles, and so I grin the wide satanic grin, I arc the high sulfurous brow, for he is in the room right now—behind you behind me: sticking his finger up your ass for a good clean dismemberment. The housecat runs in circles. The swollen glasses on the doily—everything has a respiratory system! And yet soon pretty soon, my love, with dripping armpits will come the Magi of sheep and you will be bound to stay. Friday Saturday Sunday: our first night together.*

SUBSEQUENT TO THE MUSEUM, despite the medicine, I have lost *half a head* to a migraine, a sensation similar to when you're drinking two frozen margaritas too steadily when the brain begins to throb, yet imagine this throbbing for twelve hours, although this lasted less than six; it would produce the fear of light and sound in you for you to seek the sweet quiet confines of a dark corner room to lick the newly forming eyelid of a reconciling wound, for every lunar revolution they would rip you to shreds, these swellings of the vessels in the lining of the brain, but first the feelings of displacement and then the bursting with glare, the auras, and without knowing when or where, as that bat to the head once did during the onslaught of your youth, they would aggravate the melancholy *the poetry of original sin*[11]—so whether a hangover or a migraine, whether by my hand or god's weather I drink to sober up from that other cup; they may be waning but the memory of having had them half my life still drags me around, of having them hospitalize me, so after draining a liter of wine, after pocketing four plastic shot bottles of brandy, on this early overcast evening I take to the streets already in a sweat, obscuring my own vision my glasses, only to relieve my bladder twice in the time it takes me to run between the Facility and Old City. Yet as I lay my eyes upon the gallery's façade, a mosaic mural of undulating lines and fragmentary mirror and painted tile bits cemented onto its exterior, I find myself feeling more of myself, witnessing the thundercloud looming largely like the gray and broad shoulders of a sea captain's corpse berthed upon the horizon, smeared downwardly along its fringes like cold epaulets that the soon-to-be-setting sun, albeit briefly, will brilliantly and radically filigree.

The curator spares no dispenser and evidently all the good grub went towards yesterday's private affair, a reception for bourgeois and patrician tastes, because I thought I was going to get here and find this cornucopian table consecrated by epicurean chow, the most exquisite delicacies the culinary arts could offer, rattling jugs and fancy carafes, luscious tart-sweet sanguinary wines and exotic prurient fruits and such, you know, the gourmet shit, but instead I find this wobbly table chock-full of the cheap crap, this bargain-basement boxed shit no better than the Eucharistic grape juice I used to sip at Communion: big boxed red and white wines stabbed with these little plastic spigots and a gallery brimming with these artsy-fartsy fags and pricks who you would hate to be caught dead alone in a corner with. The meats and fancy cheeses are nice though, the plebeians *are* diverse and hairy and the music sounds old and cider-scented and like it's coming out of a wooden crate. So why not? Why the hell not. I start gormandizing the hell out of everything; I haven't eaten in a day. I mean these cheeses are fucking divine: a creamy Brie with a chalky rind, a pungent crumbling feta, a porous Havarti and a mild Gouda, little square chucks of Muenster and pepper jack that people pick and poke at with colored toothpicks, smoked cheddar and this imported spread with this little red cow head on its wheel-like package, eight wedges wrapped inside these little tiny slivers of tin foil and set with these little red rip-away tags; the meats: sliced prosciutto and Molinari salami, cayenne and jalapeno sausage—and the crackers, man, my god, these paper-thin rice wafers with this wasabi sunk right in that you would think it the most ingenious thing in the world to do, sticking that stuff in, which makes you wonder why those Japs didn't win the war and you're not eating this stuff every day. It is when I am stuffing my face with these snazzy cheeses and crackers and feeding my pockets hors d'oeuvres—deviled eggs of all things, wrapped inside these little red-staining napkins—when this woman wearing a man and inhaling wine flags me down—and she is so skinny that in profile she would disappear. She, this drunken-ass white woman, just struts up with her head going *huh-huh-huh*, smirking, for she appears quite disappointed with my presentation, for when she comes up she says she's quite disappointed with my presentation. She's quite disappointed with everyone's presentation, and if it weren't for the complimentary drinks (It's very important to say *complimentary*, my dear, she side-addresses her man, a Mexican-looking painter wearing a serape and leather brown pants, a passable boy if not for the braided tail on his chin, the long braided goatee like mine, *free*, she explains, makes it sound like you're trying to get rid of something), if it weren't for the wine, she says, she would've just left—which is to say: the old bat would've just flew away; she is the typical middle-age platinum blonde who was probably something to look at a century or two ago, yet is now this great oenophilic bat wearing a much younger man around her neck like an American mink or a sombrero string. All these *blah-blah-blahs* and *so-so-sos* and I'm like aw Jesus, yet I just let this acerbic woman dump on me what she so shrewdly refers to as *the patina of tested opinion* and stop gormandizing to fix a penciled brow, as if stoically and graciously saying let me have it. So: she tells me about my work, these large-scale drawings, a pre-Academy triptych executed in cross-hatching and done in black and white ink over grayish greenish paper (a replacement for *Movement No.12*, for they wouldn't have it); she cold-bloodedly criticizes the triptych, rips them to shreds, vandalizes them with too bleak and too sad and too negative and too crowded and too this and too that—and I'm like aw fucking Jesus! Yet after she's done ripping into me, when she finally shuts the fuck up I tell her she's right, that she's absolutely right, that the drawings are indeed too bleak too sad too negative too crowded too this and too

that and that she is a *genius* for exposing me, and to my pleasure this woman's keen inebriated senses, by way of echoloca-
tion I reckon, moves right past my condescending retort for
her shoulders—the thumbs of a bat—are hunched up against
the palms of her male companion's hands, steadying her; but
then this bibulous bat breaks out and dumps on me the patina
of tested opinion to say that my drawings are just one-sided
and biased, that I'm just being inflammatory—so I unleash
the spleen! That's when this really sickly varicose hand goes
up: Oh! I'm sorry I'm sorry, my boy, but I'm color-blind. Really? I say. Yes. But you see in black-and-white though, right,
dogs do? Are you calling me a bitch! Oh!—oh no, ma'am: that
wasn't the mammal I had mind. Then she huffs and puffs and
throws her man over her shoulder her bat thumb and flies off.
Yet when she's gone, when I'm alone, I can't help feeling a
little bit sorry because I was actually starting to like her.

I may be on the piss, goes the Brit, but at least I'm not
a regretter—the one thing I can't stand is a big fat regretter.
He is the up-and-coming the feature artist, this gobby pretentious Brit with the gift of a god and the liver of a beast, a
sought-after *late-bloomer* (late for what?) who has long divorced
his wife and the suits and the day-to-day face-scrapings, who
has long stopped displaying the corporate utility vehicle (the
same hearse, he exclaims in his accented pomposity, that I had
cautiously and law-abidingly drove home every single night to
my safety-obsessed wife who was walled-up nice and tight in
our home sweet-security-serviced home on our private prop-
erty where I was routinely and sadistically ruled and bullied by
tempered imperial love and iron reason), and adopted Raggedy
Andy: the vintage clothes torn and tagged at designer prices
drapped over the feral beard-whiteboy-dreadlock-having

tatterdemalion who is blessed with a minority girlfriend and a lime green Volkswagen that he skids around town in wearing the hugest devil-may-care pair of bollocks you've ever seen, just to shake off the spleen and the nine years of alimony he is sentenced to. His five large-scale *Mandragora Paintings*—all of which have already sold for thousands the night before—recalls Donati's *Minotauro* and *Mandragore Splits Twins*, the latter being based upon the human-shaped root mythicized to have taken life from the ejaculation of a hanged man, whose scream could kill the one who rips it out, for it is by no mere happenstance that I conjure up this surrealist seeing that he just passed away this April, for he who was less than one year away from becoming a centenarian, who stated that *the fossil contains within itself all the mystery power and indestructibility of life*,[12] would be more than happy to see his seed here growing amongst these walls like wisteria. One mandragora painting in particular, *The Dismemberment of Orpheus*, looks as though a man (or a woman) is sucking on the sex of a woman (or a man) from an impossible angle—and it is so *good* that I want to throw a brick at it! It is inimitable because it transcends the medium and the technique and you find yourself looking at what's not there and praising the painter for it—O to be inspired without pollution! We should never let our education interfere with our schooling, I paraphrase Twain, and while I'm discussing this with the Brit he interjects: By the way I appreciate your drawings, being a former illustrator myself, but I think it would benefit you if you intuit more; good art comes from bad conscience, bad art comes from good intention; lose the figure; blow it out of your ass if you have to, because to understand a symbol is to kill it—and going off the point is the point of going, is it not? For once you've committed to that, mate, it can be quite the acid bath. I think it was Cocteau, he recalls, via one of his Orpheus films, who said that *works of art create themselves and dream of killing their creators; of course they exist before the artist discovers them, but it's always Orpheus always Oedipus.*[13] But then he quaffs his plonk and reconsiders, You know what, he says, don't listen to me, don't take anyone's advice. Isn't that advice? Don't be a bloody ass. But then this *wonderfully* fit creature—this inconceivable bitch built to buck—walks right out in front of us, and she seems so familiar to me but she's facing away. Do bother, says the Brit, looking over my shoulder, her pussy's on the warpath—look at the way she walks: just right for the old rumpy pumpy, huh? Yes yes, I say, returning to the aesthetics, but in reference to losing the figure to killing the symbol, and as I'm about to mention *Movement No.12* another wave of admirers overrun him, leaving me to ruminate his words, holding them up against my drawings which haven't earned a cent.

Another plastic shot bottle of brandy down, don't wretch, and for the moderate throbbing up top, a remnant of the migraine, for the ensuing hangover I swallow a couple of caffeinated aspirins. Pants down on a paper-toweled toilet seat I munch on a hoard of hors d'oeuvres, gazing about the stall, with the mouth agape with the tongue lolling and a hand limply raised, yet although I'm outside the stall of myself I can still see through the interstice, strangely aware of these engagements and yet unable to rein them in. An insipid torpor pollutes me, but then the brain begins to concoct the grimmest of heroics, some mortal altruistic deed performed before a formally dressed audience bedecked with diamonds of debutantes, viewing my life through a player in proxy, and I find myself maudlin: I don't dance as much as I used to, I'm thinking, and I'm a pretty good dæmon—I sing with the souls of my feet! But where did you learn how to dance? they're always asking me, the flowers on the wall, and I'm always saying where did you learn how to walk? I'm vacillating now between I can change my shape and escape and *I won't I won't I won't* and it is during such sentimental times when I pose the greatest risk to myself: the red decision. Immediately I spring up pulling up the pants (there's nothing coming out) and bolt for the outer door, determined to dancedancedance when I cross a lascivious lover. She is the one I saw before, the daughter of a French-Canadian Jew and a dark Moroccan Arab, Andromaque, born and raised in this city and although she's a decade my junior with a roving left eye a touch of sciatica and a venereal wart, she has this inconceivable figure and a terribly candid and ungracious way of addressing her lovers, that girlish brawn of hers showcased in a proclivity for the art of consensual rape: she is not my type, she is my pattern. The Academy failed to acquaint us with one another for she was a fourth-year student with a studio, but this past February since I hadn't had a woman in well over a year, when Andromaque encountered me sitting dumpily inside a dimly lit lounge, I was dying to be treated like a human being again—so when we drove back to her place all danced out and drunk I was anxious to get inside. She was sharing a duplex with her half-brother and sister-in-law and toddler nephew, so after stumbling around in the darkness of her downstairs apartment, listening for footsteps above, we were kissing on the couch when a lamplight licked my face: she was asking about that scar in the corner of my mouth. No no, I said, I got punched in the mouth. Are you sure? Look this isn't working. I'm sorry I'm sorry, she said—but didn't *I* tell *you* I have a venereal disease?

Yes, I said—but right outside your door! But then she told me to stand up stand up—No, over me—and repeat after her. No, I said. Why not? Don't. What? Silence must be your enemy. But before I could say anything else she was already pulling me out and was about to fill me full of blood when, *Waitaminute waitaminute,* I said, *you* don't have a cold sore, do you? And then she told me to shut up, Before I punch you in the mouth. Immersed now in *The Dismemberment of Orpheus,* in response to a flippancy on my part, a clichéd question, from a bench Andromaque arises from an underwater megathrust to reply: I see the Indian Ocean coming down like a fist. Which makes touching her seem unwise. Something has deeply altered, the sloe of her conversational eye—the one that doesn't stray—is now a pit of uncomfortable silences, having been bashed in by the butt of a bad joke, having bled out its aqueous humor and although she largely looks the same she is definitely dragging behind a mutilation on the hem of her monthly; yet there is something intrinsically illuminating about it, like a bioluminescence, for something has gone supernova inside, pulsating radiance before it collapses in on itself to the point of infinite density. She loves the way I depict sorrow, but says my drawings are a bit overblown and ask why I priced them so high and I can barely articulate an answer. Grinning, a ghastly expression, You picked the wrong vocation, she says, if you can't part with art, especially when it's not your best; you either have a morbid obsession with sorrow or a little window of tenderness you can see through—although I don't see any of the latter in your work. I mumble something in the vein of obliquity then tell her, oddly enough, that I was just thinking of her today and ask her how she's been: a week after we had coupled four policemen murdered her half-brother, the one whom she was sharing the apartment with, the Moroccan Arab's son. *We are so lonely for each other that we do the most terrible things.* According to the report, late night early morn on the drive home from his suburban security business, with a ceremonial African walking stick in hand he had allegedly rushed two officers and was shot twenty-two times. *So afraid of letting the wronged one in.* When asked why he was initially stopped they said it was for a violation; when asked why four officers were required they said it was for his hostility; no priors, nothing in his system: suicide by cop. *What has made me realize that I cannot do this with you anymore was the way you told me about the woman you had entered, brought me back to the feeling of ending, of losing the truest love I've ever known.* I ask Andromaque if she wants to get out of here, and as we're walking out to her car in the gloaming, it has rained and now is clear, I catch the curious locomotion of her swagger. *Late winter and your brother remains imprisoned, your mother's crawling up steps and you're jobless again too and my sweet sweet is suddenly a painful and burdensome love, but I hang on. I hang on and hope and live in the hope of seeing my sweet sweet coming out to me again (you having already driven across country to your beautiful mother, for I too have a mother in pain, a grandmother my only mother), and I guess you had already entered her by then, that woman, that intimacy that enter must see. My eyes lingered too, lips lingered on lips and hands wandered over me, a man's and a woman's, and thinking of you I am closed tight deep: it just doesn't seem right to belong to anyone but you. Dangerous daydreams. And then you return...*

The diner is packed and it is bright and after we eat we go next door to the adjoining bar of the same namesake to have a few. It is dark and the dance floor is dead and so I go into the restroom to take the last shot, but when I return it is like a revelry and the music's turned up like a dress and despite the sciatica Andromaque's hips are gyrating like a bacchante's at the bottom of a wine barrel, If more men knew how to dance, she's shouting, there would be less war, for with the exception of myself, in this tropical rain forest of bodies, even without the glasses and in the dark I can still see that I am the only man dancingdancingdancing—singing with his feet—while all the others are just standingstandingstanding, leaving Orpheus to his fate, to that Dionysian onslaught, to that wrath of laughter and that mirth of self-birth—to the transcendences of sweat: Goddamn it, she shouts, goddamn it! And then the scene shifts and we are veering off in her vehicle to access a shortcut that'll run us past the Facility—of course we can't couple there—and on to her place, yet as we slow down we come upon a god incarnated as a cat. It is in the middle of an ill-lit intersection with asphalt affixed to its fully black fur, the hind half oozing a liquidy black while the upper half, a crazed cobra's spectacled hood, darts this way and that, wildly ablaze by headlights and reddish intermissions—and no one knows how much is happening to it, not even an attempt with a tire or two, just cars circumventing its hisses with that post-precipitation smell, the rain having started and stopped again, enlivening the atmosphere. A plaintive and yet composed voice addresses Andromaque and without saying a word she merely pulls aside the curb; without looking at me she tells me that there's an orange plastic crate in the back with some stripped gardening gloves, yet doesn't bother to budge. Of course I have to move it first, so as I'm sallying forth to meet it, signaling a car that has the right to go to stop I see its eyes twinkling like bicycle reflectors embedded inside its head. Careful to avoid a reward of fangs I seize it, and then the body constricts, a sphincteral agony, a writhing water bag abristle as those severed hind articulations and clean fractures allow bone to swish around inside like warm chunks of ice, dejecta burbles and an evil gas is emitted, shattering my concentration so that a glove is bitten—a jolt: such a transference of fury and pain and maddening terror that like a drenched towel my hands begin wringing its neck. Cars continue to circumvent the event, intervallic headlights spotlight the tragedy, showcasing this ineffectual act, for with its spine towards me I have twisted its neck to such superb extension that its face—not a face—is facing mine, a hundred and eighty degrees of shocked vibrissae on a death mask with a mid-hiss rising mutedly in the air like a wink: Elegba is here. Àsé. I throttle it and the eyes rise. Àsé. A long-drawn-out horn swishes by—àsé—as outrage leaps from a window in the form of a fleeting profanity, a pearl of sweat plummets into its maw and the mask flickers like a wick, the eyeglasses are fogging up and I am counting down and cold and sweating and the smell and the honking and the headlights and the liquor and the peeling-masking tape sound of the wet tires on the wet asphalt—the openness of it all—makes my stomach revolt to such an extent that I have to gulp the gunk back down, leaving the nauseous tang of acidic cheese in my mouth, sweetened by the dinner's rice pudding dessert which has the dreaded metallic aftertaste of a tin bell's resonance. I return with the crate. A Cheshire cat, a silhouette with eyes and teeth and a feline physique, crosses the dim street before me to ask for spare change and I say none that I can spare and get into the car. The gloves are off and I am wiping my glasses. Andromaque is staring. Her silence scratching my corneas. Drive up Ridge, I say… *You are so proud of your pain. I don't smile enough with or without you; I miss hearing you all the time—aren't you sick of explaining yourself? I have lost the desire to explain, for do we have much more to say than fingers on the body? You thought too long, I said, because I wanted the ink that would dry on my skin to be real to be yours, to represent a part of me I am not yet sure of and so I thought of a man I might love, of ancestors whose tattoos were bruises and cut-outs of evils, I thought of Sankofa and of the sand between my toes and of the Doorway of No Return on Goreé Island[14]—and of you flying away from here in those same damn chains. And in a way I knew you would always wander wonder think (too much?), and that you didn't understand when I said that you thought too long: the ink will always be wet.*

Andromaque spots a dumpster, yet when I return she is weeping: she will take me home. I can walk from here. Are you sure? I get out. I'm so sorry for your loss, I say, and quietly close the door. It is late. It is raining. Winter before last some of us Academy students were driving from a soirée, late night early morn, when the driver clipped a cocker. I didn't see it. I was too busy looking out the window at the white moths fluttering down to cover coats of ice as the night sky swerved in a pink wintry blue bowl overturned and the streets of Logan were dead. The driver wasn't going to stop, I made her stop and got out and saw it lying in the snow, trying to decipher a motley of nightly odors with an ineffectually flared nostril before they forever vanished; it was glinting with grime, mottled by mange, its spine had been broken and before it—extruding from an orbital hollow like a tiny ball and keychain—laid a tethered eye. I asked someone to get out and help me to look around, they were white and afraid of the neighborhood, I made one get out and as I was searching around for something heavy the one who had gotten out nudged it with a discarded table leg and a front limb shot up like a rocket, and for a moment that tiny snow-padded forepaw was suspended in the frigid air before lightly lowering to snow; I could see it breathing its breath. I shoved him and asked him what the hell was he doing—he was pushing it out of the street—and I called him out of his name and he called me out of mine and I snatched up that leg, raised it, and then brought it down and then up and down for an even split. Now, I said, now we can move it.

MARE TRANQUILLITATIS

DON'T TURN ON THE LIGHT: a Sunday evening in spring, years before my final return, from the other side of the country I had paid you the visit, for never again would you be poked and prodded like some strange and withered thing by anything other than personable hands, for after two long years of battling the cancers, after two long years of being in and out of an organ donor a hospital, after the holy day for mothers my nana would be conclusively released, yet while standing in the rising night of your crepuscular room, after telling me not to turn on the light, I would contemplate the cockroach. For I would always ally the supreme hospitality of your house with the cockroach. I would imagine a legion of them—for there were many—awaiting your arrival while crawling around on all sixes under crunchable backs and hideous wings, filthy feelers fingering the creases unseen; I'd see them at night after cutting on lights, see them dart athwart the visor-green plastic of your antiquarian couches, pace over the sweat of your bathrooms' walls, over amalgamated soap bars facecloths refried aphorisms, in and around the kitchen sink, over cups cup rims baby forks and spoons and butter knives: anyplace where they could not be so easily stomped or pounded into inlay; I'd see them jump in appearance with this hiss upon the land, scuttling and shrilling a resonating refrain of fear as they wiggled their rears back deep into the darknesses of the walls. I had grown up with your cockroaches with their eyelashes on their legs, the water bugs, for the last image I have of you is of a cockroach haloing your head. However in those pastel hospital rooms I don't ever think I saw a single one in all the times I'd been in and out of that place visiting you or others, or when I was admitted myself, and this disturbs me because there are some uncivilized philosophies cradling the belief that an angel may choose anything from a child to a cockroach to come in; and if this is the case, in those crepuscular rooms, all those disgusting little cherubim are god and gone: the exterminated angels.

They had prognosticated six months: pancreatic cancer being the quickest cancer; you'd think they'd be more original. They'd chopped a year in half and made it yours and you regenerated it into four times that: the family wasn't ready. Your two years to their six months of a year (they could've said two-fourths, that's original), for you would've never let anyone know that you were feeling anything other than the utmost gratitude for a timely present, one that could keep you as long as you kept it; and during those days you were so remarkably slow to temper that had we cut off your head you would've simply grew another. I came to the hospital empty-handed because I didn't want to spend anything on something so wistful and ephemeral as flowers; besides I was sure that there would be copious amounts of handpicked highly priced beauty by the cheapest of labors and that the room was sure to be saturated and scented with a floral overflow. For hospitals are shopping malls. You are both the weeper and the consumer. Consumed by so much grief that the blood thickens and the soul sickens and the heart stiffens with the vigor of rigor mortis; the eyes roll back the mind complicates and like fists the toes ball up: consumerism soon sets in. For whenever my mother was in one, a hospital mall, I would always have to pay for her presence with gray prayers earnest appeals selfish labors of love; I would buy time for the target of my grief, buy time time and more time, the most exquisite my fear could buy, yet I would always end up peeling back the covers and the gauze, the sutures and the cause, the staple and the steeple and the open door and— look: all the little people in there wiggling around like worms on hooks. For in that hospital mall I might've been able to buy the imitation of time, a high-priced present made by the cheapest of labors, but it was a present I knew she would most likely want to exchange for something less laborious less cheapening less time-consuming than time. In the end or in the vestibule of the end we keep her present by keeping her hopeful—and it's hopeless: the saddest thing you can ever do for someone is to try to give them hope. Hope is conflict. For if we understood, maybe, there would be no need for it.

A casablanca lily a purple evening-scented stock or a hanging angel's trumpet, insidious with neurotoxins: my love, you are my flower at night. A lucifugous bloom whom I would love to touch, but flowers don't like to be touched. I am looking down and around and seeing no copious amounts of hand-picked highly priced beauty by the cheapest of labors, or any indebted relation: the room is as bare as Saturn and I want to weep. Sun setting room shadowing up and you by yourself: *My mother had thirteen children. Out of the thirteen three was miscarriaged. Do I got that right? Eight of us living and three miscarriaged and five dead altogether, and this is the order we come in: Varnnie Mae is first and she is born when Daddy is sixteen. Then there is Willis and Willis is a month old when he dies he dies of pneumonia. Then there is me. Then there is Christine. Then there is Virginia and Virginia is stillborn which is through beech*—breech—*birth, for when they try to turn her around they grip and break her neck, she has to be turned around and when they do they grip and break her neck; she's so big. Then there is George and then there is the miscarriage that almost takes Mama's life. The baby is dead inside her and they don't even know and the man keeps treating Mama for something else, not knowing she's carrying and she's not knowing she's carrying and we almost lose Mama because of the baby's poison; this is the first marriage*—I mean *miscarriage in Florida. It's Florida. After this stillnot*—stillborn—*there's Lois; she's born in Florida. All of us before was in Georgia, all before Lois.* (Thus spake the deathtape: a recording with only one voice on it, my mother's, yet somehow it seems like a polyphonic patchwork quilt of a family portrait, a many-limbed lament that I had your daughter tape and send to me out west, for the aim was to build fables based on blood, to *write* a wordless novel in one hundred wood engravings in the tradition of Lynd Ward, yet with the intricacies Doré employed for *The Divine Comedy*, for even Dante aided by Virgil had the compassion to complete his personal histories from hell. It was not that I felt lonely but pointless, for out there by that coastal grandeur and that scintillating Pacific, like a dark-winged fungus gnat entwined in a gossamer of complacency sunshine and sexual roulette, I felt a kind of howl in me by such anxiety; among those lulling land formations and that scintillating Pacific my sense of urgency was far from contextual and my sense of humor had often been embittered by the quicksand my kith and kin were still swimming in, so I had *Virgil* retrieve some stories. Those of whom who might expire soon. Thus spake the deathtape.)

I think about stealing away; you are asleep and I will find you some flowers, but as I am backing out the door I bump into nothing in particular and you stir, calling for me by my brother's name and with your voice sounding like a crumpled piece of paper pulled from a pocket book: a receipt. Never have you called me by my brother's name; everyone else does but never you. No, I say, he's in prison—and as soon as I say it I want to take it back. The static intensity of your electricity has my body abristle when I touch the pocket with the cherry-flavored taffy in it, and when I approach you with it, reaching for your lamp, my heart summits the awful expectation of seeing you lit—but then you quickly turn your head and like a bird's claw leaving a branch whisper not to turn it on. The blinds are drawn and the fading light outside barely earns admittance, but what little light does causes the cotton white nightgown to glow and the sheets become an illuminated dinghy, for from the acoustical sails of a stowaway one can almost hear the lucid melancholia of the cricket's stridulations. The light switches on in the mind then and a holy hiss is upon the land. And there would be the smell here as well, coinciding with the cockroaches in my head, if not for the taffy on my tongue. I have long stopped eating this kind of cruelty this sweet sickness, yet to ease the chemo nausea and to settle your stomach you always have one hanging from the rafters of your mouth, so I've rediscovered them to ward off your unremitting scent: you only bought a certain type of soap, and every time I slept over I would always awaken to a shower suffused with the light velvety smell of magnolias. It is a condition, something that makes you smell smells that aren't even there, hallucinations but with smells and this particular piece of taffy is the only thing that can abate the lofty tenacious scent. I carry them whenever I'm near you. And cherry. They always have to be cherry.

An entire unit is connected to your skeleton like a human switchboard as I'm stroking the human hair, hair I am so used to seeing thick or ironed and slicked back or to the sides with pomade or petroleum jelly, or simply slid under a wig, for once it became baby soft it was *it* that had prognosticated sooner than later. Scarcely can I make it out, some of has separated from the head and is on the pillow—and you might as well say what's on your mind, my love, for your ears are as big as quotation marks; or maybe you're just waiting for that day when you can finally say *unquote* since *quote* was nothing more than a cry? Even though I am shielded some by the juju in my mouth, in such proximity, your strange and permeating fragrance has the ability to leap from your pores and penetrate. I want to protect you. I want to shield you the way I want to shield the virginity of my mother who has not yet consummated her marriage to death, for whenever I imagine her without her fold-up shopping cart, waddling up walks and wheezing with quadpod canes and walkers, with pocket books and packages and plastic grocery sacks, her body, when she tries to do everything for herself I tell her she's going to fall. You're going to fall. I'm hoping for it. One day you're going to fall flat on your face and bash those bones in and then all thirty-two of those false-photo teeth are going to break up and become tombstones and fly away—Jesus! Jesus: only the son of man can understand how a mother's kiss can dislocate the jaw of a mother's man. I tell you that I forgot something, I tell you that I'll be back, that you should suck on this piece of candy in the dark until I get back. Be back before you know it. And once the wrapper's undone and it's placed onto your beleaguered tongue, once out of this room, Christ, I run... *After we move up here up north, after Lois, then come Cynthia. Cynthia is born in this city. Stanley is born in this city. Shirley is born in this city. Then there is the miscarriage she has at the same time Christine is carrying your cousin Nadine, and this is the second miscarriage when Mama falls down the steps and loses the baby. No, this is the* third *miscarriage she has when she falls down the steps and loses the baby; the second happened before Shirley—we don't know what happened with that—and the third happens after her. So that's us. There are eight of us living and three were born but died and two miscarriaged. No, two was born—or rather one was born and the other was almost born—and* three *was miscarriaged. That's...that's thirteen? Let me see...ten eleven twelve—yes: the thirteenth was the one that fell down the steps. That was over on Van Pelt Street...* Your womb was a tomb: where are the flowers? It is Sunday night and nothing is open: the streets are as bare as Saturn and I want to weep. I want to wail. I want to wiggle into a deep dark bushy possession and I curse and go back, but when I do I see the kiosk inside the atrium. Upstairs the room is lit and you can't speak because of a tube sabered into your mouth, the taste of cherry is lying on a paper towel beneath a florescent tube and the skin is darker, darker than its usual hue, darkened by medication—and she is telling me the nurse that that can't stay here, that flowers aren't allowed in intensive care. And yet from tenderness or intubation your eyes are glinting aquatically.

———————

I AM NOT ASHAMED OF YOU: you were home when your second daughter said it, said it during a cleansing and in truth this is how it all begins, isn't it? This is how it all ends. The truth of humans and water: I will keep you dry and out of the pain was the promise so fragile it could barely be spoken, and that night with a guardrail down and your hand grasping her breast you wept onto your daughter's chest. Yet keeping you dry was not always a promise capable of keeping. At night under the lullaby of morphia you would empty yourself onto yourself and be totally oblivious to it; soundly would you sail through a menagerie of dreams only to be moored by morning in a corrupt adult diaper: the woman who was so used to doing for herself for over a half a century was now reduced to being the sunbaked tummy of a turned-over slug—with the heat and the humiliation cooking you constantly. The second daughter, exhausted, would sleep on the floor at the foot of your bed as soundly as you, while her father would've been coaxed from the couch to the single bed beside yours (the king-sized bed being discarded), for you needed an adjustable bed whose foot and head could be raised by remote; yet he would've never slept in the room with you without his daughter, he would've never faced his fear—at least for the time—of you dying on him, so when his daughter slept over he would sleep the soundest of you all, and there wouldn't be the slightest sense of smell astir. Yet once when dawn broke and the daughter awoke to smell the misdeed and see her father gone she shamed herself and said she was sorry, but you—soaked and fetid—just smiled to say there was nothing to be sorry about.

Changing you and your sheets were a routine ordeal, so before doing anything that would require moving you or invading your privacy you were given the option of morphia, so that the cleansing could be an act of love instead of an act of torture. Once the needle was laid upon flesh the soft and yielding spot would gently suck it in, yet as the daughter knew this the injection would feel like a scalding-hot board smacking your bare wet bottom, so she opted for alternative modes of administration: a drop under tongue or a suppository. If music was wanted music it was, if gospel was needed gospel was given. For my love, I am rolling you over. This is what she knew to do, this is what she knew to say even before she was told to say it, Always let your patients know what you're going to do, said the hospice nurse, before you go and do it; rest them assured; and while your daughter is rolling you over in my mind I am sucking on a piece of candy in the dark while watching through the crack in the door: *Thus saith the Lord God unto these bones...I will lay sinews upon you and will bring up flesh...and cover you with skin and put breath in you and ye shall live.*[15] The palimpsest of your final sheet of skin is as ancient as the verse impressed upon it, and after you're propped against the upraised rail, the other being lowered, the nightgown is unbuttoned in the back and opened up for me to see that the medicines are so strong that the unveiling not only reveals flesh and vertebra but ulcerations: bedsores have proliferated in spite of precautions, like being powdered down and rolled onto your sides every hour or so on the hour or so. After the fitted sheet is removed, while lying on your back, the gown is pulled off and inside out to expose the jagged shoulders of a concave torso, past the pubis and legs and off the body entirely to expose the sorest and ghastliest of sights, the vision of the valley of dry bones: twisted arthritic nodosities, a forest of joints, impermeable bone-hugging flesh, sideways-fallen angel breasts as shriveled as turkey wattles and a puerile floral-printed diaper woven wholly of cloth that is worked free to expose septuagenarian genitals and tossed quickly atop the flat sheet that is currently on the floor. A mightier smell of despoilment fills the room and I receive it with such volatile clarity that I whisper the very mystic question the Lord asked of Ezekiel: *Can these bones live?* Only to answer: *O Lord God, thou knowest.* Yet after having stolen from the hallway and into the dark adjoining laundry room, holding my breath, I am watching your daughter move towards the bathroom to fill two plastic basins with assumingly warm water, drop in one two terrycloths and the mark of your tallow soap, and then toss a towel over her shoulder to bring everything bedside, leaving your door lastly cracked. I am seeing the sanitary feature on the floor, a massive oblong shape that has taken on a semi-gelatinous composition, for is to be removed and disposed of later as something spoiled, whereas the diaper constructed of cloth will be laundered by hand. After a terrycloth steeps the water and is lathered with soap, after it is wrung with such a pontifical grace that it grips you, you wait for the blessing to ensue, the acid bath: For my love, I am washing your face. You close your eyes for the ghost to glide the hand-contoured cloth across it, wiping it clean of earthly torque, and then the second terrycloth is taken to the body, one basin becoming cloudy, I suppose, while the other is inundated by rainbows—with the shriveled flesh of your sex being rightly left for last. Water alone will be used to let the body do what it does, cleanse itself from inside out (for I've done this

before with her, the daughter performing this for you now),
and when you are rolled onto your side you are wiped from
front to back—never oppositely: *culture* can result from wiping
oppositely; and as you're being doused now with cornstarch
powder I can hear the row in my head: That's something a
child would say, I'm saying, women having *Petri dishes.* No, my
father's saying, that's something a *man* would say who watched
his wife give birth to three yeast infections, three pussies. But
now you are being alternately rolled onto your sides to be dia-
pered and gowned and for the mattress to be fitted, for the
white plastic has been wiped down with disinfectant, heralding its gleam of sanitization as the sun reflects onto the ceiling
the aureole of a soft silhouette. Finally you are tucked beneath
a fresh flat sheet like a geriatric newborn and inside a clean
cradle you lay and I have to say, I have to ask, What was it
like, my love? What was it like sleeping on the floor at the foot
of her bed and then trying to rise—when you can barely bail
yourself out of your own? And sitting beside your daughter
now, on her bed, she tells me that she had to use your bed as
a crutch, that the carpet was grubby and steeped with mildew,
that she heard mice and was tickled by cockroaches, warped
by the unyielding hardness of the floor, that she had to limp to
the bathroom or because of great pain go on herself, that she
hurt her own bones crying all the time, But I had to overlook
the pain, she says, I had to overlook being uncomfortable so
she wouldn't be. Keep her dry and out of the pain was the
promise. But I couldn't sometimes. And that hurt the most.

———————————

DAYLIGHT SHOULDERS YOUR SIGNIFICANCE, sketches in sepia, for
inside this sketchbook evanescence is bested, all my mistakes

are in ink—for how can you know what is superfluous if you don't know surplus? How can you know if you've gone far enough if you haven't gone too far? A cool moderate spring today, curtains flung wide open, yet only the vesper sparrow can unfasten this lucifugous bloom; you have been given room blood bath medicine and are now flattened with flat sheet tucked so tight about the neck, body so desiccated, that your head on the pillow seems separated and serene, guillotined, when I see it plain as day broad as daylight: a seraph: from the far end of your headboard towards me it crawls, a conspiracy of legs, and then it rests as a sedentary terror above your baby-fine hair your medically darkened skin and your open and closed eyes; on the nightstand there is an open container of blueberry yogurt and I am frozen in disgust, unable to move unable to crush it, for you are wearing a disgusting little crown and I am utterly dumb. For it's looking at you at me at you, sharpening its antennas together, until it creeps back behind the headboard, knowing the score like a notch... *Wanting to take your lifes and wanting to stop the pain ain't the same thing. Wanting to stop the pain is just wanting to get out of the misery. I know I been there. People don't want to take their lifes, that's why you take that second dose—not to kill yourselfs but to get some relief. It's okay though. I always say we're just pilgrims passing through, just pilgrims passing through...*

Your table will be ready. For while listening to the tape I see it being set. For after two long years that were tough as nails, a week after your hospital release, without your consent your sanction you are to be finally absolved of the body, and the very woman who will relive you will be the very girl you saved from a table gurney long ago—so she powders and perfumes you, forgoes the diaper (They're drying, she says), dresses you immaculately in a white nightgown as the sad and shriveled effigy of your former self, administers the taffy, and then shifts you onto your side so that the gown can be hiked at the hem. The burn then the hot wet slap, the surfeit of morphia, and in the deepening affection of the afternoon sun, resplendently peering through the windowpane, as children shoot each other outside with their forefingers and call each other out of their names, with a steady gaze you are watching your room molder from a head-raised position until it completely disintegrates and you are seeing yourself sashaying into a sea, or suiciding in an ocean, until that too disintegrates and you are seeing yourself strolling barefoot along the red clay lands of the southern savanna, hand-in-hand with the baby brother on the lone distrusted road of red dust, and you are looking down at his face as his honeysuckle thumb falls and his eyes balloon, so that now *you're* looking through that undulating drapery, through that seething curtain of heat, to see what he's seeing: the liquidy shimmers of the golden white calf, half-alone, crossing the red road before you on the wiggly-line legs of a haint before descending into a red clay ditch which you, having proceeded to, discover empty. The sun blinks. The children are down the street. And from your mouth the taffy is removed and dropped inside a crystalline jug of water to dissolve at bottom at best, where the rich red syrupiness, rising in misty swirls, will settle soon enough.

She was my best friend, your second daughter says; I used to take her everywhere. Her goddaughters were there; they were sitting on the stoop. My seventh sister too; she even wanted to wash her body again and when she asked why she didn't have a diaper on, only underpants, I just said she didn't want one. You and my second son are the only ones I ever told; my firstborn sees in black-and-white and my older sister wouldn't understand, not that kind of pain; none of my sisters would; she was just coming over the bridge when I called her and she had to pull over because she was peeing herselfs, crying so hard. I was cooking eggs and grits before I did it, just upped and went into the room; never did finish. She had no appetite anyway. Hard to swallow… *Mama would never do it. Mama would never do it to herselfs, not on purpose. I didn't, not on purpose; wasn't what I wanted: the doctors did it first with their morphine and I did it with mine—both of them was accidents. Those migraines was just so hard, you know; came in clusters like brown bats. If Mama had a hard cancer and couldn't carry it I wonder if she would want me do it. Or do it herselfs. I don't think she would, not on purpose; she just so proud. I truly applaud her. I never saw my mother cry. Only times was back when we heard about Sherette jumping off that bridge and Nadine being hit over the head by one of her boys' daddies. Mama had raised Sherette after Varnnie Mae left Harold, raised Nadine too. She had four boys, Nadine, and Mama wondered about that, if those boys had grown to think about it: about one of their daddies murdering their mama. He stuffed her in a trash can and didn't do no time. Even wanted to come to the funeral. We would've knocked* him *over the head and threw him into that hole…* Everybody touched you. Except for your second daughter's second son everybody came by, even the ones who weren't even born and those who have long left. All of us came by at different intervals from six in the afternoon to nine at night, filing past your bed to kiss and stroke you; everybody touched you; we never covered you. Yet when the hospice nurse came in that ambulance bearing those duplicitous marks of theft death and deceit, the wands of Hermes, caducei which would've been more appropriate on the blind sides of a hearse, when they pulled you into that black plastic bag and zipped up your face…that was the worst. A sight to behold. And then Medicare came for the bed, came straight to it to take it apart and take it out. The service was held at your apostolic church and when we buried you in the cemetery your second daughter's second son wasn't there either; we couldn't afford it: he had to stay in there behind all that human-proof glass and steel and deal with himself alone. My father surprisingly showed up and everyone was laughing and crying and showing some symptom of god—except for his eldest son…and your third daughter too, our neighbor now; she didn't show much either. Didn't even cry at her own daughter's committal, Nadine's. I never know what's going on inside that woman because she never shows it. I don't think she's means it; she's pleasant and smiles enough and has long taken on her five grandchildren and now the great grandchild, an endless consignment of kin, but she will never show you a drop. She can't afford it. We can't afford a marker. It doesn't matter though; no one ever goes out there anyway. There's not a flower on your grave, my love. Not one. Not even from me.

She's not out there, I'm saying to your daughter, she's not out there buried beneath some plot of dirt—she's not. During her attacks of grief, during the pangs of nostalgia, as if I were a lover I kiss my mother on the lips. Today on the holy day for mothers she is poring over photographs while listening to the tape when I, sitting beside her on her bed, lean back and cup her face with my hands to take in the totality of her: It is not so much that she is gone, I say, but that you are left. And as she opens her mouth as if to say something dreadfully important to me I slip in: We're just pilgrims passing through, remember? Just pilgrims passing through. And already, as I am saying this, I am getting up to leave.

LACUS MORTIS

I AM HALFWAY THROUGH. I have just passed the candelabra and you are growing larger. You are embedded inside an encrustation of undyed linen, impeccably white in contrast with the pure darkness of your skin, the grayness of your bargain-basement suit, the blood red slit of the silk tie and the black shiny shape of the open casket, ruffle-brimmed, with lid interior lined impeccably white as well. I see a titanium-colored bar along the length of it, and where your feet are there is a white sheet hanging over the side at a right angle like the drape of a tablecloth or a dinner shirt untucked. No: you are blackberry pie filling a raven a personification stuffed inside a dough-frilled pan and waiting to be covered with more of the same, waiting to be pushed inside flame and hellish Fahrenheit. Yet on the threshold of this long bright room I first noticed the eleven chairs, six on one side and five on the other, how they're spaced to support the walls and no one else: the walls would've followed me without them, I know, come closing in like a compactor of condolences upon every step I took towards you. There were only four provisional lights on, two electric candelabra in the middle of the room, rising from opposing walls, and two tall standing lamps at the far end, sentries or doormen you could say, one on either side of him who has already passed through. The elderly man the pink-white man who prepared you, the director, had asked me his patron for his pardon as he moved to turn on more lights, two fluorescent overhead lights and two more lamps between the candelabra and the doormen, no doubt thinking that one should have more lights when viewing the beloved—as if a flood of wattage can lighten the load of the weeper who is also the consumer. Don't, I tried to say, don't turn on any more lights—my god, I don't want to feel like I'm in aisle five with flour and pie filling with sugar and spices and panic attacks, yet already he had, turned them on, and this makes me resent the old faggot. Although I know in my heart of hearts he isn't severe he's effeminate, mottled with rosacea and aging and kind with clean cuticles of conscience, with almost a half a century of soil in his blood in this business—yet also I sense upon his fall of silence fresh cries crushed by the tight-lipped mouth. For what? for whom? who knows? But it is for this reason and this reason alone that I'm purchasing his services. I am the weeper. I am the consumer.

Standing over you I turn: sitting beside the entrance is the director in the twelfth chair, separate from the eleven, and this too makes me resent—no *pisses* me off: I want to be alone with the body, you fuck. You should know. Forty-five years of accommodating customers, you should know. But I don't say it because there are already those ten pristine fingertips shaping a form in the back of my mind, harboring a heart, and then the white snowcapped skull I see and *Saturn Devouring His Son*[16] so avariciously that I long to scream into the white sheet and to swallow myself with sleep. I return to you. Other than for the faux nose, fired clay persuasively painted, it is how it is always imagined, isn't it? The whole body lies in impeccable taste: suit and tie, (lift the sheet) shoes shined for the shoeshine boy at heart, a skillfully trimmed mustache and—wait? What? I asked for the goatee, you were growing a goatee, you never grew one I have one—why didn't he keep the goatee? He asked me if I wanted to keep it and I told him to; the firstborn was sitting across from us at the restaurant table; he heard me. But of course: the firstborn. That was why he walked the director out into the parking lot while I stayed behind waiting at the table, the lastborn waiting for the banker firstborn to return and *settle the estate*. What estate? He walked him out into the parking lot to tell him to take off the goatee; he had no right—he's jealous; everyone wants the dead to look like them. Although face to face, mirror to mirror, I am recognizing the resemblance: I am looking down into that face (without its glasses and without mine) at my face (not the firstborn's face) mirrored a million mirrors away—and I find it hard looking into the face of the dead when the face of the dead looks like me. Your eyes are going to open up and grab me, I just know. Yet deep down down deep, elicited from this facial tranquility, there is an utterance in me, a word an unpronounceable word which I can only here pronounce: Papa?

Your leg is so hard I start crying. Stop. Turn: the director is gone, removed from his seat and this makes me respect him even more. Respect? Resent? The difference is the same. I don't know why I touched your leg—whim? magnetism? force of nature? Never even touched your legs in my life, never even thought to. No. I touched one once before, way back in our house, grabbed it really from the side while I was down there on my knees, frantic: I was bawling with snot seeping out of my nose, crawling around on all fours, naked from nap to toe with swells on my back swelling, my arms my legs my face, puffy strips of leavened flesh the width and breadth of a man's belt and you wearing as always your white V-neck T-shirt—naked from the waist down—with your manhood showing. You were wild. While you were ripping into me with leather I seized the leg closest to me to get closer with your savage uncircumcised sex dangling overhead as if it were the Sword of Damocles on a string of horsehair, and hugged it tight real tight, hoping you would keep beating me, hoping you would breathe harder so that in crazed exhaustion you might make a miss and sting yourself instead. Or retire. It is so hard, the leg, like a block of wood. I knock dully and cry again, choking sobs; it is so hard. Once more I move to lift the sheet. Look at your shoes. I need shoes. I think of taking your shoes.

Before being moved through this long bright room by some postmortem magnetism, while in the lobby of the parlor, I asked the director to take me to the room where the body was prepared, for after hearing about your adornment I was a little resentful that he had ignored my original request: the day before at the restaurant table, as a student of anatomy, I had specifically asked the dotard to let me see my father unadorned undone denuded: I've drawn from dead bodies before. Well, I almost drew from one once. I was set up in front of it and everything, easel out supplies splayed paper prepared, and with the overhead light on full blast to help lighten the load with the stark commonness of a grocery aisle when it dawned on me: I'm supposed to be somewhere else. I was supposed to be over in this really finicky faggot's apartment, a real flamer a painter, we were supposed to be posing each other in the nude and already I was five minutes late and across town. Let me see. It is June. It was last December—during the end of my future—when after studying the works of Tisnikar, an alcoholic empath, a deceased Slovene mortician (*The Painter of Death* he was dubbed, for he had only painted the people he prepared as he imagined them in life or in afterlife and only with the murky aqua and earth tones of his drab slab room), as a first-year student, I was able to pull some strings based off my talent to visit the medical research ward associated with the Academy—a privilege reserved for third- and fourth-year students; and after wheeling out the cold cuts of a cadaver, after peeling back the pale leathery skin to study the inner mechanics of a thigh and leg, I found myself sitting down there in a basement with a winter jacket long johns and a ski cap on, ready for the long haul, but as I was trying to make my appointment, as I was pushing this body back, a pale Boricua with an algae-colored ring rounding her neck, the crime of passion, as I was trying to push this big curvaceous body back into this big rectangular container of broth this female attendant came in—and I don't know whether it was the fear or the formaldehyde but I had to pull myself together because I was crying. I didn't say this at the table of course. All I said was that I'd drawn from dead bodies before. For this is something we have in common, I wanted to say, but didn't to the director: I'm a draftsman of the human form and you're a restorative artist, a man trained and skilled at molding human features from wetted clay to be fired in a kiln then cooled and painted with proper pigmentation, for use as a nose that had been bashed in or a hand or an ear that had been snatched off to console the inconsolable, to forever embed an unblemished image into the hearts and souls of them, for those finely crafted faux noses and ears and hands will be more than capable of weathering the underground or the vaults as bone pottery, or simply given back to flame—although never annihilated: either or your exhibitions will always be for one viewing only. Instead of mentioning this common interest I just said that I was a student of anatomy, because after asking if I could see my father unclothed undone denuded the director's facial features appeared quite quirky to me. There was no food on the table, I was proper about that (although the director wouldn't be eating anything anyway—even so his stomach must be extraordinary), and I don't really care about the firstborn: all I knew was that I needed to see it unclothed untouched unaltered in order to properly work the craft. Were you very close to your father? the director asked me, right in front of the firstborn who just kept his hands folded atop the table, and I said yes. Yes, I was. Close enough to choke him. So no I did not mind being frank, nor did I think it inappropriate, my father was my father and you would've minded me seeing you naked in death, for I had seen you exposed in life.

I am stroking the human hair. The only human on you. It is as soft as a babe's and yet was wooly once, stubborn with nigger knots naps in the kitchen, and stroking it I know you must be smiling: You are the only man, you once said to me, who I ever let stroke my hair. We weren't fighting we weren't drinking we were just sitting and talking and smoking cannabis dipped into embalming fluid inside one of your many shitty apartments, and on your bed over scattered textbooks and an open holy book (you were studying at Geneva then, a seminary) you talked about god and life and loneliness, about your fear of being misunderstood, about how your dream was to have your grandchildren cry and throw up on your breast and how you wanted to die while changing your clothes and dart for the sun like a diamond; and before I left you asked about this drawing of mine, this densely cross-hatched drawing of a bull elephant head with a graven image of a calf lodged in his forehead, but since it was a drawing I had made for the mother, instead of saying that I couldn't offer it to you or even offering another, I just stroked your hair in the doorway and we embraced. We kissed. It was a holy kiss. Full of what may be betrayal but what may also be blood. I let go and the next time I would hear from you would be over a year later with a background of screaming on my end of the phone and a background of screaming on yours, both bedlams bickering across our conversation, for I was on that island of a city that monstrous American city in the one of the five boroughs, working in a residence for the retarded, while you were a resident at a sanitarium for the insane: it all had something to do with a girlfriend and her son and you arguing with him, a live-in in his mid-twenties then, and the son running out after you with a blade and you getting hit by a car and the cops showing up with a nigger or two on their tongues and with you being you and the cops being cops you were beaten and detained, yet instead of jail your biblical rants had enrolled you into a laughing academy where you were crucified and twisted back into shape—at least for a time—by the sleek boneless words of the nubile nurses, by the unprofessional humaneness of the young black doctor who reminded you of your second son, by the flying acrobatic tears of the old white man on the bed beside yours with lice in his beard and dandruff on his pillow, by your bipolar counterpart who had just lost his only daughter to salvation which led to starvation during a religious retreat out there in the desert wilderness of the Mojave, a fanatical purging for forty days and forty nights which reminded you of your baby sister Omega who had died of malnutrition when you were in the ninth grade, of how you cut class and cried, wandering down north Broad Street until an aging preacher, a white man, caught up and decided to wander with you.

The eyes stray and I see the size of you when full of blood, your *membrum virile*, and how sensitive a prepuce might've made you and I wonder about this, being circumcised myself: if I could've been more sensitive. I want to touch you I want to hold you but I'm afraid you might've been petrified. There is no smell to you and your hands are ashen, crossed over each other over the belly, and when I place a hand over them they are the same average size: on the white-hand side of these dark philosophers these gardeners of thought there are the dark-lined fortunetellers who—after a foreseeable slap—would turn the color of sunburn on the palest of whites; but the body has been evacuated of blood and the fingers are wrinkled in contemplation, still centupling some tender touch: The sun rises and falls on your mother, you once said, during a time of low, yet as softly and swiftly as you said this you made a sincere accusation against her fidelity. I accept the similarities but our scars vary—and look: the nails are uncut. Dirt has crawled underneath. As if already you are trying to find a way out before you are even in. So: even in death you're dense. You're not going into the ground. I'll make sure. My father is going to burn.

There are two rings, one on each ring finger as though you were wedded to two opposing personalities: the right ring is from Geneva, encrusted with a sparkling sapphire a deep purplish blue eye surrounded by an island of pure silver, and the other is from the College of Bible, the first seminary, fourteen karat gold and encrusted with an unidentifiable scarlet stone; over twenty-five years ago my mother earned you that ring. You were working a lot. You were a foreman in production control at Meddle Tool & Model Company an all-black company owned by a white who had lifted you from a blue collar to a white, from a machine shop to an office chair, for you were humble he had said. And so your wife had to study for the both of you because the two of you were enrolled together—yet you denied this. Men rarely say the truth, she said to you, unless it's to back up a lie, and as I'm pressing a cheek against your chest I can still hear the same dead silence in response. Such a good heart a feral heart a wild organ of anguish and play, until it had to undergo a surgical procedure and was attached to an artificial pacemaker, almost at the precise moment—the very high point of the obsequies—when your own father was being lowered into the earth: the two events being only an hour apart. You never got to see your father's funeral; you were too busy dying. It would be several days after the fact while sharing a hospital room with a saved suicide that you would break down to call your stepmother only to hear that your father was already rooming in the earth, but then she would tell the firstborn and he would tell the ex-wife and the ex-wife would tell the second son and me—yet at separate times the ex-wife and the second son were the only ones who went to see you. After years of being crippled and alone that woman had hobbled down there to see the only man she has ever loved, but you were sleeping, and when she came back the next day you were gone. The sun rises and falls on your mother, you said, during this time of low, for you were convalescing in a transitional home for addicts and homeless men and after years of living in a house with a spouse in separate rooms, bound by mortgage not marriage, years after its foreclosure, you had finally yielded to my request to ask her out on a date. But then you backed out. Yet before we found you in the hospital we didn't know where you were. You were missing. When we wanted to find you you were nowhere to be found; we feared you were being stubborn or bipolar or dead. For it's easy to miss someone when they're missing. It's hard to miss them when they're not gone.

How heavy are you? I am thinking you were about five-ten and two hundred and forty-five pounds in life but in death you must weigh a ton. The director told me back in the preparation room, a large glaucous *shower stall* postered with exclamatory signs and equipped with wall tiles exhaust fans and drains (I was preparing to see you), that for every high index of formaldehyde, for every sixteen ounces of that noxious gas mixed with a cocktail of arterial fluids, preservatives germicides anticoagulants dyes and perfumes, it took a good portion of water to work them throughout your entirety via veins and arteries and to expel them through your jugular by use of a heart pump and embalmer, a Crockpot set on a black cement base with a round white gauge dark star-like dials and a long rubber tube attached to a needle—or something like a needle—hollowed out like a viper's fang for easy insertion inside the neck's carotid artery; and since sixty-four ounces of these eternal fluids were required it took a good four gallons of water to complete the feat. Your system is completely depleted. The inflexibility of the body is perfect. Not all the water in the world can save you now, nothing in you is unduly rotting, nothing in the body or the lining of the belly itself is harboring even the tiniest of organisms, not a single solitary drop of fluid exists: everything has been flushed out sucked out siphoned exsanguinated. Not even a leftover fart. Only the weight of the empty. He weighs a ton, the director explained, his skin is as tough as a leather belt and every muscle and tissue is firm and hard and over time will get even firmer and harder. Your leathery hide will cheat and retard decomposition for a good number of years and the worms will have to wait, but you're not going into the ground, in spite of what the family might say, in spite of what the firstborn has said. You left me in charge. Not him. And the second son's away so he'll just be happy to see the body—if we can pay for him to see the body. Our earthly father will go up in smoke and there's not a goddamn thing they can do about it. They can call me a heathen or a bastard all they want. But I am a heathen and I am a bastard.

LET ME SEE. It is June. Last December during winter solstice, while revisiting the other side of the country, I was with you over the line and listening or rather not: you were going on and on about how humble you were after I had just explained to you that I was assaulted by four men and three trashcans in less than two minutes, all over a look that had raged in me much too bright: a considerable part of my lower lip had been hanging, ripped by a ring, but I had bitten off that ribbon of flesh and swallowed it so that a nice young specialist would have to reconstruct it by using the nearby pliability of the skin; however an epicanthic fold, an eye smooth and puffy and pulled at the corners, was like looking through the chink in the blinds and the hematoma from the trashcan's impact was like wearing a ghastly gigantic package over my head, for although the head was sutured up quite nicely, I suppose, it was still swollen beyond anyone's imagination, except for yours: Head look like a wedge of cheese, doesn't it? Over the line I could smell the felony of your aftershave (You can take the boy out of this city but you can't take this city out of the boy), I could see the receiver dripping embalming fluid from the body of the blunt (You ain't ugly though, you just beauty turned inside-out), and to make matters outstanding the glasses were broken. I couldn't see shit. I have horrible eyes.

Cradle of the Panther.[17] Medusa Marie's metropolis. In a friend's flat, in the northern section of the Golden State, east of Merritt Lake, I was listening to your oblivious mouth while pondering the predicament of my face my lip my head, for I was self-effaced, having backed into the bookshelves the paper bins the whole study I was in, for I could clearly audience the symphonic movement of my molecules mending, but then the mind rebooted and started replaying in several serrated snips the night of the assault: drunk and cold and riding a bicycle I had rode to her once-favorable window, sweating and panting before an obstructed driveway before closed curtains, just to hear my dear sweet Medusa Marie in the rhythm of heat, under the thrust and smell of another and with his hand no doubt cranking her neck for her tongue to lick his tit, with her moaning ad infinitum without any asthmatic fit, moaning for me with *his* name and with him posing as me saying the same: *Whose whose whose*—my god! I would've gone mad. I would've done something if not for that little something in me, that little voice that prevents a man from going insane or committing suicide or murder. I couldn't hurt her. I couldn't hurt him if I knew it would hurt her. I was stuck, wanting someone—anyone! But having no one around to fuck to get unstuck. And so cycling back to the flat, through the wind and the cold and the dark, I rode by this nightclub, out of business, and found what I was searching for—although you wouldn't have been able to convince me of it at the time: a group of like men at like time and need, four beasts with one human head or were they one man with four beastly heads—yet without heads: mindless skull sockets without any boundaries or lines to cross? They were gripping voluptuously shaped paper bags to their mouths as their backs clung to the cries of a weeping wall, a graffitied memorandum of the neighborhood dead, with the ache and the *alc* blooming in their head, preparing them and getting them ready for the common intent of which they themselves were conceivably clueless about; and that little voice which I thought was preventing me from going insane or committing suicide or murder was nothing but a little spreading stain of guilt, and that little bit of guilt—unlike a lot—was too much of a pussy to outright let me hurt myself, so I had to get someone else to do it instead—without cognizance. And in doing this, in getting someone to kick the ever-living shit out of you without letting yourself onto it, a sort of psychological sciamachy you see, you can feel a little bit better for feeling worse, because it is a hell of a lot better than feeling a little bit of guilt. All I had to do—and you wouldn't have been able to convince me of it at the time—was pedal my little ass down that street and let a primitive treatment take its course, let one of them look into me and then I would look into him and then he would look harder and then I would look harder and in these long seconds of commerce there would be lifetimes of hatreds and hungers and humiliations exchanged; he'd call out to me—shout—this headless-headed beast, a vulgar name a pet name he brands his woman in heat, and in the seconds it would take me to stop and turn around that bicycle, with street bravado, I would have already answered his beckoned call by staying on this train of thought and not jumping onto another. For we attract who we are. Not who we want. I don't remember much. You know how these things go. A lot of posturing and shouting, spitting and what have you. Yet before all of this I remember seeing this beautiful ebon woman whom I didn't see at first, a sort of shadow with eyes and teeth and a feline physique, but when those big beautiful pair of eyes swimming in a Dead Sea of sperm walked over to me to say, Hey, sweetie, if I were you I'd just get back on my bike and pedal my cute little-ass home, all the while palming a piece of paper into my hand, I was utterly aghast; and no matter how helpful she thought she was being, even if later she wanted to fuck me blind, her words had a mortifying effect, as if she had just reached into the front of my pants tucked my dick between my legs and told me to hold it. I decided against going anygoddamnwhere threw away that piece of paper and continued to stare at my marked beast, men of my size and stature, and after all that spitting and posturing and shouting and what have you one of them came up to me and was so fast or I was so drunk that my mouth exploded, and then I was catching a quick gold gleam of that great gold ring, cocked and ready for another. I didn't flinch. I just stood there: as a child I was taught to never flinch; and with those wraparound stems even the glasses were in place. The man looked stunned though, embarrassed even, as though he had expected me to fall down and stay down with one punch; he staggered backwards himself and I asked if he was alright and I guess he took this the wrong way because when he lunged at me the second time a foot caught him clear in the chest, floored him, and then his bulls, the other three, started laughing and laughing, the way that boys do, so when he came at me the third time an instep turned those legs into a tuning fork, caught him clear in the crotch. I wasn't doing anything. It wasn't me. But before this puppeteer could pull me to punch his clock the other three, armed with three gigantic trash cans, descended upon me.

I remember more than I thought: blood oiled the spokes and chain the sprockets—misplaced passion everywhere—as I was riding the friend's bicycle baptized in blood, and from where it was springing I really didn't know. There was no pain though, even the cold air felt good, and I remember having a hard-on and hearing the shouts of that girl lying to them that the cops were coming, for after they left me staggering around that deserted street, lolling my head and drooling my tongue, no cops ever came. I don't know what happened—Christ, I came out of the *womb* drunk, slapped the doctor and everything. But instead of my temper I'd lost my interest. Or maybe I just got tired of hitting myself, for one of their faces started to soften. The main problem now was that the glasses were broken—they had *repeatedly* hit a man with glasses, you believe that? I couldn't even see it to believe it. I was cycling and cycling through the dead of night and I couldn't see a goddamn thing save for my recent oversight. I was thinking I have no money, they took that; no medical, not in a while; so instead of cycling to a nearby hospital, at least they left me that, I rode to the friend's flat that was several miles away.

Yet away she was for the week. So I was alone. So that now I am making my way towards the bathroom, treading bloody sneaker prints across the kitchen tiles, for I have come through the backdoor to avoid the living room carpet, and once I peel off the blood-drenched fleece jacket and shirt I grab a green towel from the knob behind the door; yet when I blot and blot and blot, the red-green conjuring up the old yuletide melancholia, the bleeding doesn't stop, so that now I'm thinking of the raging level of liquor that's possibly thinning and preventing it from tying a competent knot, for after all I did fight the good fight and bike a good ways and there's no doubt that the heart has probably pumped every ounce of that poison throughout my entirety, so that now I am in it for the long run: temporarily incapable of clotting and irreversibly high on my own blood. I step into the bathless shower stall with the white porcelain base, for some of the blood has dried already, leaving the hair—I have hair—coated with crust and the neck scabrous, and beneath the showerhead I wash and wash and wash and as I look down between the two big toes, gazing into the pink swirling centrifuge fixed above the drain, I become dizzy while feeling around up there through bushy blotted blood-matted hair, using the fingertips to tentatively comb the side of my head until I reach the breach the opening—and then I realize that something irrevocably horrible has happened to me: with a single solitary fingertip, marveling my own existence, I am touching the raw and throbbing part of me that has had every neuron in my brain relocate a good portion of the body's blood to that locality in a desperate attempt to try to address the problem; I find edges, two or three ragged flaps of skin and hair and—why I don't know why—while standing under this balmy umbrella of water I peel back the edges and look down to see something so hypnotic and serene that you would think Saint John had saw it: the water at the bottom of the white porcelain base has drastically turned into a deeper shade of red, and I—pouring profusely—am ankle-deep in it. I fly out. Call her, I'm thinking, let her know let her know how much—let her know *that* much! But then I think of the moon. Of how it looks up there tonight: like an illuminated fingernail clipping. Then I think of her nail clippings littering the outside of her windowsill—or maybe they're his? Maybe *her* nails are at this very moment digging into the very density of his back with her damn ankles tying down that bow around the small of it? Maybe he's biting down on that thick thigh of hers, close to the cunt and the femoral artery—and with his incisors leaving the very visceral marks in which *I* to leave? Or is he biting down on that shoulder?—good god, that shoulder: as smooth as a doorknob and as soft as an au revoir. How she used to fuck me! I thought *I* was fucking her. How she used to scream scream scream after that skipping-record rasp, after that lesser asthmatic self had been cast off for that out-of-body experience—how she *wanted* all the time. How confused I was— brother wolf and sister moon! How she pounded me to death. How she pounded and punched me through the bottom of her bed with her bush and her pain and her unadulterated disgust for anything that was not love or of love or love-like or love-ish—and I'm pissed: after all these years, standing here fauceting blood, I am finally realizing that that cunt was trying to kill me. I decide against it; I'm not calling her—I don't want to *ever* suck those dick-sucking lips again! Then I think of my head my face my lip, of how it's hanging and fall to brooding: who's going to kiss me now? I think of calling her again but call a taxi instead, yet no one will come to this neighborhood at this hour—and I haven't any money. I call a friend and immediately hang up: he's a dæmon and I swore I would never get into that death-bucket again—you need a goddamn stunt-double to drive with him. I call at least three more people I know, but no one's around, no one's awake; it's late. I can't afford it. I haven't a choice. I have to call an ambulance.

You shouldn't have bitten off your lip, they're saying, the doctor and the specialist; we could've used that bit, but we'll make do; it was probably dead anyway—and I can't comment, really, because my mouth is strapped to this offensively expensive machine. You lost a lot of blood, they're saying, the doctor and the specialist, a bucket or bucket-like or bucket-ish; they admire my fortitude, how I could ride a bicycle for miles take a shower and wait for an ambulance and not faint. I motion for them to remove the muzzle: Anger and snow, I say. Anger and snow. And then they look at me, this doctor and this specialist, quite coldly because I'm practically on the Californian coast, during the yuletide season no doubt, not in the *Spirit of Despair*, but I guess a good portion of these people have never really been in snow—I mean been raised in it lived in it waited for the fucking bus in it. They don't deal with extremes. To them other than for strapping long flat sticks to their soles snow seems pointless. And since it's sunny most of the time and rarely rains it's safe to say that California is wasted on Californians, or maybe they're just thinking I've lost a lot of blood and am up here on Magic Mountain, lightheaded and talking shit. Yet when the doctor and the specialist leave this East Indian woman, a trainee, stays behind to take a blood sample, and she's from my city by way of New Delhi and says that my vein reminds her of the Germantown arterial: it breaks off just to pick up somewhere else inconvenient. But already

I am back at the friend's flat, staring into the quicksilver of the bathroom mirror, looking at a lacerated lip while recalling a childhood adrift in daydreams and absent-minded states of bliss, chewing candy while molesting my mother's earlobe and while the trainee is drawing my blood, inside of this preparation room, I am playing with my own earlobe and while I'm chewing on my lower lip. My mouth is dry and my eyelids are heavy, yet after she's done the trainee turns around and says to me, East Coast people have stamina, West Coast people have faith, and with that being said she just silently removes herself from the room.

(After reconstructive surgery, compliments of the extra efforts of that specialist, six months now after the assault the bottom lip has fleshed out quite nicely, leaving only the line going across the middle and the cold sore-like scar in the corner, and although the hair has died out in places the gash on the side of my habitually shaven head has settled down into a nice flat memento: a wishbone or a letter of the alphabet, an upside-down Y pointed heavenwards, a celestial configuration sired under the sign of the Sagittarian arrow. All in all: I'm just happy I can tie my shoes. And Medusa Marie, what of her? She never even knew I was in her city again. I think of her all the time now, of her smell of her olfactory profusion of snake-like locks coiled around and up over her face, under my face: a pillow smell of aspen and rosemary deep inside the primordial brain. I miss sleeping with her. I miss sharing sleep. The same heart rate. I always liken sharing sleep to two cottages resting upon a hillside somewhere, in open country, both having windows and doors, shutters and screens, flown wide open at night and sometimes during the noon hour to allow the other access into their house of dreams…god, I want a family. I want a family that will save me from family. I want a daughter, even if she has asthma. I want to be a normal person, even if I have to be...like everyone else.)

On the line while lying in the friend's flat I was silently saying to myself that it was a suicide attempt after all: suicide by assault. I had tried it before flying home the final time—at least that's what the television tells us: suicide by cop. Was this what I had? Was this the actual intent and not some unconscious need for social readjustment? Yet it never ceased to amaze me how in the friend's flat, after all my wanderings, that you didn't even notice that I had been silent for a good thirty minutes or so, saying not a word moving not a muscle; at one point I even sat the receiver down, yet when I picked it up again I just heard you going on and on about how humble you were in the South, about how you were a Freedom Rider, about how you had marched with King himself and was bailed out of jail by Thurgood Marshall, about how you had been driven out of Poorbuck—or whateverthefuck—and into the woods by some sheriff and some citizens for trying to desegregate a diner, about how you had to think on your toes by reciting Psalm 151 at the mountaintop of your lungs over and over again until the sheriff couldn't take it anymore and told them to leave you alone on that chair under that tree in that noose, about how you on your tippy-toes and wrists bound behind your back had to wait to cry for help—which, I suppose, came in the form of a buck-toothed chipmunk—with your only living relief coming from the long urinary trickle veining down the burning of your inner thigh and calf. I stop you right there. Psalms stops at a buck fifty. And you start ripping into me. Those rants of humble milkings curdle into slanderous spoils, into clouding-dumping maledictions, and the man who has given me the six tongues of a revolver and the tail of a rat is relentlessly tearing into the woman who has given me my six seraphic wings, calling her *Antichrist* and *Satan's whore:*

She a whore! You don't know what she did, son, and you don't want to; I spare you. She a whore and you a pussy. Your mother raised all three of y'all to be pussies. I'm a man, jack, a *man*, and you either got your head in the clouds or up your ass.

You know what…where do you live?

You think I'm afraid of you?

I'm coming home for Christmas, I'm coming home for a talk, and during this talk if you have something to say I'll let you say it, but if you happen to say *anything* against my mother—I swear on my eyes—I'm going to punch you in the heart.

You think I'm afraid of you?—bring it on, jack! I've been through all kinds of shit; I've been beaten up by cops crooks robbed choked shot—punched through walls! You think you can kill me?

I'm the only one who can.

Don't give me that crap, you my son my seed; I brought you in and I'll take you—

I'll be back December the twenty-fourth; I'll see you December the twenty-fifth.

You better have the Word of God in your heart when you do.

I'll have the word of god on my fist, and it's going to be your fault if you open the door.

Hallelujah! Hallelujah!

Hallelujah.

You love me?

I want you to die.

You mean that?

YEAR OF THE RAT   97

With all my heart.

Fuck you.

Fuck *you*—you fat black jiggaboo bastard!

You fucking little cocksucker—you call me that?

No, I'm calling you a charcoal afterbirth—*that's* what I'm calling you!

You fucking little faggoty-ass-faggot-pussy-dick-sucking-on-Satan's-tit!

Then hang up then! Why did you call?

Fuck you *boy*.

Where do you live?

I'm not afraid of you, you boy you punk you—

Where do you live?

I'm not telling.

I don't want to know.

You love me?

Don't call me again.

I love you, son.

You're like herpes…

I love you.

You never go away.

You love me?

Call me again.

Family quarrels are bitter things, they don't go according to any rules; they're not like aches or wounds, they're more like splits in the skin that won't heal because there's not enough material.[18] On the fourteenth of June, in the year of the rat, five weeks after your sixty-fifth birthday, the day before the fathers' day, my father the dæmon who loved god received a permanent cessation of all his vital functions due to a massive heart attack: you were found face-down in a filthy apartment, four flights up with no elevator, clenching your chest with aspirins and cereal oats split on a carpet steeped with spilt milk, rotten eggs rationed on a kitchenette counter above a broken-down mini refrigerator and your glasses—from falling face-first on the television—crushed and your nose shattered. But before you fell, in the hallway at your neighbor's door, your last heard words were: Can you help me, son? And I see you clenching your chest, hunched over, standing in front of your neighbor a boy barely a man and with his doorpost holding you up, and you are gasping and sweating and your words are barely audible with a tablet of glyceryl trinitrate dissolving under tongue—and I find it fitting: fitting that such an explosive personality would become so direly dependent on nitroglycerin. I am standing over you. Other than for the faux nose, fired clay persuasively painted, it is how it is always imagined, isn't it? The whole body lies in impeccable taste: suit and tie, (lift the sheet) shoes shined for the shoeshine boy at heart, a skillfully trimmed mustache and a sutured mouth appropriately plugging a forked tongue—yet it is opening this mouth, parting as I see you staggering back to your room to wait for the ambulance and I cannot misplace the image of the door being cracked (Can you help me, son?), of you lying on the floor (Can you help me, son?); why is the television still on? Can you help me...? I wish I could turn it off...

MARE CRISIUM

Could it think, the heart would stop beating.[19] We are consciously living in an interregnum now. I say *consciously* because—although we have been in it for some time—we are only really living it. The father isn't going into the ground, I tell her; I'd bury him in front of our house if we had it, but that's the only plot of dirt I'd put him in, for it is her presumption that he would not want to be burned but embosomed by the earth. Yet he would've never named me the head of the will if he wanted this. You should bury him. When was the last time you saw your mother? You should bury him. I know what I'm doing. Don't do it out of spite. Sparring partners refusing to capitulate, negating each other, we play it out in front of the parlor not far from the Facility and—aside from the cousin who identified the body—I am the only one to have seen it, to have autopsied our relationship, his character, yet as I stand against the mother under this weather-beaten awning, a stretched-out sun-bleached piece of skin powdered by light now the color of ash, incandescently diffused, like a contrary antacid I find my resolve dissolving inside, removing all relief to such a judicious degree that the mere thought of cremation turns me ashen. Overhead a curved arrowhead a flock formation wheels towards the earth. Surmounted by strati is a mock sky, gossamery gobs of cotton spread thinly inside my second-grade shoeboxes scene, a continual scene of eight linking rectangles ambitiously forming an octagonal city, viewable in the round: its post-bicentennial decadence, its smokestacks and oil refineries, its tri-state traffic and exhaust carbons begriming the sky and lethargizing the blood—yet with all those ambulant mouths just jostling about to fill in the moonlike potholes of its streets with their superfluities of words. An edentulous day today, I am thinking, full of persona and void of bite, a toxic ennui. A black-feathered bird with an iridescent sheen preens on a Washington Hawthorn and is chirping now, using *her* panpipe to call for the epigamic coat of a mate. It is a morning that neither expresses nor impresses anything, yet she is dressed to impress, a long-belated date and I am chauffeur and chaperone: she is dressed in a two-piece outfit, a black blouse and dress printed with pastel corsages, oranges and yellows and reds almost as bland as the day's palette; the hair's dyed auburn, cropped short and cottony—yet when the wind kicks up her perfume is singing the warlike hairs of my nostrils, a noise in the nose a miasma savaging me with all these romantic excuses and ruthless compassions combined in a kind of canary-yellow pheromone: Jesus! I say, how much did you put on? A few pounds, why? No no, the perfume the perfume—I can't feel my *feelings* with that shit! Don't you curse me! I'm not cursing you! *Yes*, you are. And then her face crumples and her shoulders slump and I feel like some nefarious lump in her throat. I'm sorry I'm sorry, I say, kissing contritely the greatly dimpled forehead of the girl playing possum, I'm just...you know? Yes yes, she says, it is too much, isn't it?

I try the knob, I knock on the door, and despite tapping respectfully the reverberation has enough hollow-wood sound to smear the gesture with an echo, yet not enough stain to desecrate the sacrosanctity of the place. I try the knob again with the same right hand and find it only turns clockwise: life goes on. Yesterday the door was wide open and the lamps lit along the small partial wall of paperbacks—a peculiarity within itself—seemed to have turned the lobby into a living library where the spirits of the bereaved could be borrowed by the deceased to be later returned to the shelves of themselves, either unscathed or with marginal markings engaging their principles—except in those sad and precarious cases when they are not, when they are pocketed to go limp and dog-eared with compunction in such possession. Aside from the mother's yawn the lobby is undisturbed and dim. Today it neither looks nor feels like a library but an accommodating aquarium awaiting sea life, ventilated and replenished by cool watery air emissions, contrasting the outside humidity and one's body heat; and it is this union of the two temperatures which has me wiping my glasses and then hers, and after replacing them I simply ask if she wants to sit while I search around. No, yawning, no, eyes gleaming, teeming with sentimental terror, yet under halcyon waters now, with quad-pod cane and her heinie like a fin, she undulates into the watery den of the parlor. Time seems fossilized underneath this artificial ocean floor of silence, this long quiet dark, and through the glasses the enameled night at the other end of the room is obscuring the portentous delineations of the casket, yet the softly glowing white sheet and the *indivisibles*, those eleven ethereal wakers in their wall-checking chairs, grow finer and brighter with yielding pupils. We hear a sound a whimper and turn to our right: there the director sits in his twelfth chair, separate from the eleven, with his skin phosphorescent and his elbows to his knees and his hands across his face. Is he…? Yes, he is. The mother sees it too, so we quietly retreat to the lobby where a chair groans taking her weight. She draws in the longest yawn yet, so after switching on a small discrete lamp I remove the pouch from purse, the black pouch, and after pricking her finger with the pen-like device, after milking the speck of blood, I scoop it up with the test strip jutting from the palm-size doodad to read it: her glucose is low. However as I'm preparing her insulin needle I find myself thinking of the director, of the partner he mentioned the youngest son, who after the double birth of his daughters, quadruple Geminis, only deals now with the business side of death: no more for him, not after his cherubim. What is it like embalming babies? You must have to have a heart of Teflon and a surgical fastidiousness to build such sailing ships to ease inside those impossible bottles. Will the son at least have the heart to embalm the old man his reverted child, to send him off with reputation? What sacrifices has his father made to allow his children their pink complacencies inside the shallow thinkings of their birdbaths? What is the sobbing about? Did Papa touch him? Did my reckless solicitations, did my prying into the postmortem cosmos of my father hatch some maggot in his heart, some larva to wolf the dead tissue? However as I'm straightening her top to tuck in the fifth tit, the insulin having pacified her yawns, the overhead lights jump on and the director emerges from the dark scared waters with this hieroglyphic look on his octopodous face, the rosacea a complex network of pink suckers enclosing the lobster shell of his red lobulated nose, wearing the slapdash consolation of a coral-colored-gummed smile, feigned imperturbability typical of the *fluid squirter* inked by pathos—which taints the tender image of having just glimpsed the man naked in his heart. She's come to see the body, I say.

The room is flooded once more with the bright indifference of a superstore, and after the director sits at the entrance I am escorting her along the length of it, lengthened by guilt and grief, handicaps hers and mine and with that manufactured scent just trailing like a bridal gown; and when we reach the far end I pull up another wall-checking chair alongside the one already here, sidling up against the man-size jewel box to mind her silent appraisal. The father is presently hanging about himself as a purple aureole, and with the whimpering eyes of a pup the suit looks up, quietly complaining of unholy texture, his skin. I check his nails—he cut his nails—and though merely an amender I am moved. He looks so quiet, she says; he's perfect now. Like he had to lose his mind to find it. Like he had to spend his whole lifes becoming his best friend. And then she goes quiet, the kind of quiet between chapters, those blank spaces of what now? *I have lost friends, some by death…others through the sheer inability to cross the street.*[20] Well, she crossed the street and still lost him, because I crossed the line and punched him in the heart. *Death and Life are in the power of the tongue, and they that love it shall eat the fruit thereof.*[21] I leave her to him and head towards the entrance, to where the director offers his seat, and protest as I may he ups and leaves anyway. Pray from afar. I entreat my game my blood my mother to bestow upon me some cohesive grasp of her depth, so that I can pounce upon it with some level of objectivity or with some object of affection—yet nothing but this deep bottomlessness I can't contend with as those animalistic emanations loom largely from the perfumed seam of her thyroid wound. I watch her back tremble imperceptibly as her head bobs between her shoulders, and then after a moment I see the head cock and the shoulders pump: she is laughing noiselessly now and I can almost see them buried together, not apart but together, down there under god's green acre, juxtaposed beneath a bed of begonias with lumps and crumbs of dirt plopping onto the attaché case of a backgammon board, open to a game. And even now there is a part of me looking back to see what I could've done differently, but the problem will always remain to paraphrase Jung; I will need to outgrow it instead of solving it. But I cannot resist the temptation to *do* something, even if this something is just to pull out this arrow of sorrow by pulling it in deeper, by getting it over with—which is why I left the Pacific in the first place: to get it over with. For there is no such thing as an old wound. Sorrow is always fresh. For whenever the pain is entertained *I am* sorrow, and I cannot sit with this without trying to separate it from myself—which is why I never get it over with. Regardless the lights are on full blast and I find it hard to study in a room obliterated by brightness. Never trust a room that doesn't cast any shadow. It'll bring down a night darker than one that does.

YESTERDAY THE MOTHER THE AUNT AND THE COUSIN who identified the body began the clearance of the father's apartment, so that today the firstborn and the lastborn are the final leg, siblings who—except for the row at the restaurant (and the grandmother's committal)—have neither seen nor vented the spleen with each other in over fifteen years, so as we're riding en route to the father's apartment I take in another good look at him driving his sedan, at his portly body, only to hear the mother calling again from years ago: I am back on that island of a city that monstrous American city in the one of the five boroughs when she calls me: the firstborn at twenty-seven, after having undergone a tricky rerouting of wiring, is now the youngest patient in the history of the hospital he is in to have survived the bite of a heart attack, and I am listening without listening, remembering what the aunt the accountant, the one who will scrub up our father's blood, had said to him while he and she and the mother were lunching. He had just moved to his adopted city just west of his natal city when his heart, perhaps, first started missing the beat, for the mother had called him weeks before out of a last resort for money, money for new teeth, because she was she edentulous and pathetic and looking twenty-years older and not twenty-years younger like she usually looks in the face—she was looking twenty-years older than her time when he told her he'd call her back. And never did. So that now: Oh! we're doing fine, he replies to the aunt's inquiry, smiling amid the grating perturbing sound of tiny serrated teeth sawing porcelain plate, quartering his medium-rare sirloin as the salty red grease and the pink juicy core, contrasted by the burnt umber of the sirloin's surface, makes the blood pressure of everyone at the table rise as their deaths their dates sit down. The wife and I are blessed, he blathers, truly blessed;

we've acquired a really great house in the suburbs, I started working in a really great bank, and the wife's a secretary for a prominent attorney—the Lord is blessing us, truly blessing us. Pause. The kind of pause his aunt permits whenever she's waiting for you to say everything you have to say to say, Are you sure? The mother's face wilts towards her eggs and grits, bacon bits in butter, slowly masticating the mush with a kind of bovine inefficiency, for not only does the dentures rake the gums but each chomp is like the dark clop of a hoof. Am I sure? he chews. And then she fixes him: Are you sure you're being blessed? Since then he has had two more heart attacks with the last looking so grim that the doctor told him to call his mother. The bypass has brought about terrifying bouts of breathing and his groin—a porn star's—is being lathered and shaved on a routine basis, for a balloon-tipped catheter to be slid through a coronary artery for imminent inflation inside of—what would otherwise have been—his strongest muscle.

The sedan pulls up to the father's apartment, but as I take in the interior again, the plush fresh-leather-plastic smell the tinted oculus of the sunroof and the computerized consul gracing us with every possible amenity down to the controlling of our bowels (an upper-echelon office with the head honcho here commandeering the helm), the numerous jalopies our mother has been contracting over her long inextinguishable life, that cavalcade of auctioned-off autos, parades before me—and then I am guilt-ridden about not collecting enough capital coddling children, sad about the second son being away (yet even before he went away he was always just too busy getting there); so that now the mother, tottering on spavined horse legs, rides a subcompact whose engine wobbles like a die, yet it is her wheelchair, her major mode of locomotion, and if not for the handicap license plate a single city block could level her. Regardless throughout the city's center where the doctor's office is, with its sparse parking and calcified laws, over time she has accrued fine upon fine which cripples her even more, and then those *two* city blocks from the doctor's office to the garage have to be taken for the sobs to make the pharmacy in time. On the way back once she fell. Two teenagers had to pick her up and place her onto a curb like a heavy fetid sack, soaking wet, and when the ambulance came like a sanitation truck, because of the smell, she couldn't lift up her eyes.

Entering the father's apartment we see a shopping bag from the old neighborhood shopping mall and I remember my hopes of purchasing an action figure, falling upstairs to get to my piggy, when I broke a plaque. It was Sunday and although the father was always angry on Sundays on this particular Sunday he would be the angriest. To begin where do I start? For one to understand the barbarity of the father's affection, in order for one to feel the spare-the-rod-spoil-the-child, one must first feel the significance of his favorite trophies and plaques: inside our house and below the main staircase numerous bowling trophies from an avuncular tabernacle—a place of worship now nationally known, founded by a paternal uncle and yet fostered by the father and mother—would perch atop an upright piano caked with dull primer paint besmeared with dirty oily fingerprints and a drop of dry blood where my chin had blossomed following a D'Artagnan vault over the banister. The bowling trophies with their calcitic bases of crescents and squares equipped with metal stabilizer studs had plastic Corinthian columns hoisting up risers indicating first second and third places and wooden and marmoreal tiers topped with crucifix-crowned spires and head-wreathed figurines holding *cranker* and *stroker* poses, glorious bygone Euro-looking specimens, plastic Olympians once lionized and stamped with hot metallic foils of imitation gold who were now shouldering the dandruff of mendacious make-up while frozen in high backswing. Utterly incapable of letting go of the golden years they would continue utilizing *late-timing* to reach some nonexistent foul-line, planting-and-pulling with seal-like bowling shoes, using no slide whatsoever, and to draw the most *oohs* and *ahhs* by leaving the most spectacular splits they would cup their wrists and bend their arms to keep their hands behind and up under their balls for maximum rotation. The plaques were lined along the staircase wall as lacquered walnut rosewood and cherry wood testaments of unassuming service, with those shield-like shapes and squares affixed with imitation sapphire marble ruby red and black brass design plates, all delightfully laureled by an engraver's stock vignette. Plaques certificates and awards, outstanding memberships to councils associations boards and committees, recognition and acceptance emblazoned by calligraphic lettering and lasered into the father's head but never his heart, substandard and yet cherished acknowledgments from his reverend his brother his surrogate father. Yet all those plaques had their jigsaw puzzle parts glued and re-glued, replaced and re-replaced upon their wooden underpinnings depending on how many times they were broken, for they were always so insidiously hung along that staircase wall like mounted mousetraps. *Comely my brethren were and tall, and yet they found not favor with the Lord. But I, I sallied forth to meet the alien and he reviled me by all his idols. But I drew forth the sword that was beside him, I cut his head off with it, and from the sons of Israel removed reproach.*[22] On the father's box spring I am reading this supernumerary from a Septuagint, the very apocrypha he had used to tame a necktie party, a passage from Psalm 151 relaying the slaying of Goliath of Gath related by David the King. I am now setting aside the milk crate of remaining plaques when the firstborn, exasperated, squeezes through the door his lumber of flesh, and it is much easier for a camel to enter the eye of a needle than for him to enter the kingdom of the heaven—for heaven and hell are positions of the mind and not places for the soul. He is wheezing, wearing a jumpsuit, sweat glands pumping at peak capacity after having lumbered down the steps the television that broke our father's nose, the big grumpy box of dirty clothes loaded with wide-waist underwear mottled by spores (I'm surprised he owned any), and the mattress soiled with semen and splotches of Rorschach coffee stains in such near-bilateral symmetry that one can—by way of psychoanalytic algorithms, I suppose—expose that underlying thought disorder or that particular sarcoma of character; he lugged all that crap down four flights of steps down the hall into an alley and up into a municipal dumpster so *doggedly* that I'm equally impressed, so as he's bating his breath, bending over his knees, I feel a soft rustle in my heart, some sentiment in the bush which electrifies my affection—and then all my resentful resolve dissipates: I am so used to seeing him stout not sorry, fit not flabby, all those years of beef and grease, of pig flesh and electrocution from a transvenous pacemaker, of his tentativeness towards exercise has finally cocooned him in such a meltless mound of yellow cow fat that I pity him. A cunning on my part. I touch his arm and I am static-shocked by a thought, by a flash of him clutching his chest, of a nurse's aide and a can of shaving cream, of the child he'd been trying to beget for years sobbing over his breastplate and of her first word becoming the last he hears. I tell him that he should clean the rest of the bathroom while I take down the rest of the stuff, for yesterday after taking an hour to hobble up four flights of steps and rest, as not to jeopardize the full deposit return, the mother had scooped up double-bagged and disposed of the father's raging two-day-old dejecta from the backed-up toilet by dispensing it out the window into one of the dumpsters, so that the unpleasant part is over. The box spring slides next door to the neighbor who rang the ambulance. He is young enough to be my son—if I had a son at sixteen—and aside from a rancid mattress an egg-encrusted hot plate and an unsettling television on top of a black cast-iron stand, an archaic arachnid, his place is about as pleasant as a spritz of pesticide in the eye. The boy tells me that the father was wearing only a white V-neck T-shirt when he came to his door…and that he is sorry. Sorry for not letting him in. Sorry for letting him die alone. I give him the recliner the recorder and the audio cassette tapes—all except one: a recording of the father singing to his first granddaughter, six or seven then, after his second son's arrest: imbued with ambivalence for having survived the bite of a heart attack and yet bereaved of a father, a man who had never really loved him, he sang in the empty visiting hall of the transitional home for addicts and homeless men. He sang a song of unconditional love for one's self with such a reticulated baritone that—during those self-exiled years from his brother's tabernacle, as a fisher of men—he could have easily ensnared a congregation for himself had he truly embosomed it. Returning from the neighbor's room, next to the leftover possessions in the hallway, the firstborn is conferring with his wife over the phone, safe and sound with their baby in their city, wearing latex gloves as not to smuggle a pathogen home through the receiver holes; and as they

quibble over imponderables without even quibbling, over in-
consequentialities impracticalities and incidentals, you know
the future, they quell these very undercurrents of conversation
with hypocoristic lapses of conduct. I walk past him into the
father's apartment for the last time and genuflect inside an
empty closet: after rampant narcotic pursuits and edentulous
prostitutes began desecrating our house our father, a decom-
posing patriarch, began hiding in closets. After his wife and
sons had successively vacated, after the desecrators had scram-
bled in, he emptied out all the closets and installed internal
bolt locks for fear of police raids—for a closet door locked
from the inside could be a competent deterrent. He prayed in
them as well. Called them his *prayer closets*. And in *this* prayer
closet, in this silent marsupium of agapé, I bet for forty nights
by working the knobs and cracking the door with their sala-
cious big toes various starlet-disguised harpies of the porno-
graphic profession—the crème de la crème crowned with cal-
lipygian profiles cupped by the kitchenette's stove light—must've
tempted my father with crack pipes the size of laboratory sets,
to lower himself by exposing his hindquarters for the culmi-
nating mount of a toy. However no witness to any freebasing
had ever come forth on the coroner's slab: my father had simply died from a supreme sense of false confidence.

The devil's proof of purchase is in hand, the tithes-and-
offering envelope, the selfsame lunch money envelope that had
never came into question by me until it was found unaccount-
ed for in the empty bottom drawer of my mother's musical
jewel box—where it had always been expected. The envelope
is proof of the father's lust for the church bride, for status and
acceptance inside of the house of the holy—a house he had
helped hoist. His brother his surrogate father, a reverend torn

between the Bible and the bedsheets, had overslaughed him
on so many occasions that—for a whole year—he stole from
tithes and offering; however after being caught and dismissed
from the deacon board that same year he was brought before
the board again, this time for writing an anonymous letter
regarding the reverend's alleged infidelities with the church-
women; and although this letter was written and sent without
his consent by his firstborn son, after denying writing it and
yet maintaining the son's anonymity, after refusing to accept
the public apology he chose to leave for good. And—without
knowing any of this—it was on this Sunday when I was to
go to the mall with the monies I had saved, it was on this
Sunday when I would break—for the umpteenth time—one
of his favorite trophy plaques, it was on this Sunday when I
would receive word of a celebrated singer slayed by his father,
a man of the cloth, with the same .38 caliber handgun the
son had given him as gift. I swear on my eyes a second before
the plaque falls he yells my name; upstairs he is sitting on the
center stage of his cedar chest as some prerecorded sitcom
is sucking him in headfirst, a live situation comedy similar to
the situation of the Minotaur or the Hall of Mirrors, where
one is repeatedly lost inside unvaried syndications of himself,
and in anticipation of my pre-recorded appearance a hyper-
realistic applause is cascading down the staircase while I am
looking down at those broken pieces of plaque the mouse-
trap, while the television dinner is squirming around inside,
cooing curlicues amid the imaginary teleprompter's blinking
red lights and pre-recorded applause, arguing and wadding
its way towards my fundament like a drunk towards an exit.
I'm upstairs now: Take off your clothes, he's saying to me,
calmly coolly, sitting upright in his stark-white undershirt that

is contrasted with the dark nudity below—and my expression earns more applause more laughter more echoes of platitude, yet before I can say anything, without looking at me, he just tells me to take my clothes off again and since he isn't wearing his glasses, since I have perfect eyesight, I can clearly see the shifting light of the program gleaming inside his pupils: a walleyed delinquent sits on his Meddle-Tool-&-Model-Company-constructed linen chest, watching a sitcom while I'm wondering if this all is some sort of farce, if the mother and the second son are not just in the other room, chuckling, instead of outside waiting in the car; I'm crying and crying and he's telling me to shut up to shut up to shut the fuck up before he gives something to cry about—which makes me hysterical; he stands then after I'm done undressing and lifts up the pants of his Sunday best, perfect down-the-middle creases, and then whips out the leather so fast that I barely have time to react: the first crack goes across the back for me to relieve myself (APPLAUSE APPLAUSE), the second catches a cheekbone and an eyeball goes all crazy (APPLAUSE APPLAUSE), leaving the exposed lamp bulb behind his head zigzagging across his face, so that now the third going across the crown (APPLAUSE APPLAUSE) is merely aimed for rouse; I am scampering around the way a rabid dog does; the beating intoxicates him—I can see it in his eyes: for although the television has been turned off and the pinhead has faded to black the program remains. I shoot for a leg. He kicks me off and I crawl for a closet. I crawl for the undergrowth, for the dust-settled spikes of her shoes and for the cotton-woven forest of her clothes, and as I'm enclosed now by the overwhelming smell of perfume and piss, mothballs and shit, he tries yanking me out by an ankle before springing to his feet. They're shouting.

He's ripping into her. He's crisscrossing her with *whore whore whore* and she is crying and calling and fighting for me to get out to get out to get the hell out and dart for the door, which I do with her hotly behind—yet as we're falling down the staircase, breaking plaques, he can barely stand by the bedroom door, crying with an erection and reduced to his domain.

In an idling car she is sobbing into her hands not knowing where to go whom to tell what to say. The second son is in the passenger seat asking what happened what happened and I am in the backseat saved from a fire, wearing his shirt; my body is burning, the sweat-stung sores, and the plastic seat upholstery is so cold and clammy it's kind of creepy: I am wearing only a white V-neck T-shirt...and I smell. Are we going to the mall? I say. But then I feel my face and it isn't mine anymore, and when the second son turns around, in the streetlight's glare, I don't need to see what he sees because I see it on his face. The interior light cuts on and I shut my eyes, clenching his shirt; she tells me to take it off and turn around and with eyes closed head down I do. It is only a few seconds before she's facing front again, but when she looks into the rearview mirror, when our eyes roughly meet, I can see that her face isn't *hers* anymore either. And then she is holding it together again like a wet grocery bag.

Hours later the firstborn enters the house, the mother having sent him to a friend's, and he comes into our room, the second son's and mine, looks me over and then lowers his head. To get to the bathroom to apply a balm we have to pass by the parents' door, wide open, and I know now that the father is far less fond of him than he is of me. In the dark the mother feigns sleep, careful as not to lie on her bruised sides with a bread knife under pillow, while the father, wearing his glasses, is sitting on his cedar chest like a sepulchral piece of art, wearing his usual while watching the day's programming conclude to the anthem of our country when the firstborn, my banner man, parades his monstrosities before the door by pausing my person. Yet when the father simply returns to the television's radiance, wearing his reverend's frames, it is only then do we see how forensic-blue lens can fluoresce offenses unobservable to the naked eye.

THE CLOSET DOOR IS PULLED BACK. What are you doing? I'm praying. Oh, are you hungry? And remembering the row at the restaurant, without looking at him the firstborn, I simply say that I don't have much of an appetite. Yes yes, he says, you always had to be a little hungry. I pack the remaining parcels of our father's possessions into the sedan to redistribute later, but as the firstborn is driving, taking the roundabout way to the Facility, he passes through the old neighborhood and I become angry: two days ago I had asked if he wanted to take the short drive down with me to the nearby county—thirty minutes away—where the second son is being momentarily detained until his private viewing of the body (his last-minute reprieve having come from a former protégé's transport payment), and the firstborn in his matter-of-fact way of manhandling matters had said that he still had a million things to do: wasn't *he* the one handling the affairs? But what is he doing now, taking me on a trip down memory lane for some sentimental ambush? The sedan stops in front of a gas station mini-mart, the scene of the crimes: there is a cenotaphic telephone pole on the corner riddled with oxidized staples and standing in memoriam to superimposed homicides: withered flowers and faded photos,

tattered teddies and discolored hearts, deflated-in-spirit bal-
loons and a cluster of laminated bereavement cards all dripping
with grief and regret, encircled by a séance of melted-down
multi-colored candles that you would think people would stop
stopping here. I need copies, he says. He needs copies of the
death certificate, copies of the will, copies of each of the bank
forms handling the estate (yes yes, the father had an estate),
leaving the firstborn and the lastborn (the second son having
already been bestowed by the city to the state) over thirty-three
thousand dollars—before the angel of taxes of course—in
checking and CDs and variable annuity for a three-way split
between Shadrach Meshach and Abednego, for the father will
surely be the angel in the furnace soon; he needs copies of
the notarized renunciation document stating that the head of
the will has signed over the whole affair to him (with the strict
stipulation of cremation), for the branch manager of a downtown bank will surely need to secure a short certificate from
the city court in order to set up an estate account in the father's
name; he needs copies of all the receipts of all the expenses:
the filing fee the mortuary fee the cremation fee the church-
usage/repast-preparation/presiding-pastor-honorarium   fee
the columbarium-plaque-complete-with-porcelain-picture fee
the inscription fee and the book-shaped-portmanteau/instal-
lation fee (the safe deposit box for the cremains and its armored compartment—two per double niche—inside Ivy Hill
Cemetery), totaling ten thousand one hundred and sixty-three
dollars and seventeen cents that, my god, death doesn't dis-
turb me as much as the documentation. I would rather deal
with tangibles. I would rather deal with the three of us in a
room together—after fifteen years—than deal the rigmarole
of death, yet the firstborn just segued into this whole affair of

cremation, that it's an abomination and paganistic—not like that of course, said it slick-like, but I know what's two and two. He's just upset about not being the head of the will. Yet *am* I doing it out of spite? Am I trying to get back at the father or his family? All he ever wanted was to be accepted; maybe I just know that what I'm doing is right? That no one will ever get out there to see a burial site. But here I am about to burn the father and it never even occurred to me that I'm going to have to burn her too, despite her wanting to be buried, for she would surely want to be beside him. You can't burn one and bury the other, you idiot; the firstborn understands this: two per double niche. And it is this understanding—more than his acquiescence—which makes me feel the fool. But then again: the dead always give the living the nicest plots, now don't they?

There is a line of dark birds clipped to a billboard advertising a motion picture franchise whose *sequels* are prequels, and as we're pulling out of the mini-mart a child darts across the street and we barely miss him: days after the mother and I were skinned alive the firstborn tried to suicide. I found him in the basement. When he had grown tired of the noise the arguments and the responsibility he moved down to the basement which soon acquired the maturing musk of his adolescence, along side that already-stagnant stench of runoff collected in divots around the washer. Down there those several cereal bowls of talking toasted rice would be left atop the television set to get soggy, and the only time when we would see him was when we did laundry. He was asleep, I thought, not *asleep* asleep. I tiptoed over rat shit and held my breath, but as I was opening the dryer door as quietly as I could, from the light in the laundry room, I could clearly see the barbiturates beside his bed—and after several waking attempts I simply ran upstairs and got the father. I started calling him a girl after his stomach was pumped, yet this ideation started before this really, right after the second son was born and right after the mother had mowed down that boy: the firstborn was in the passenger seat being a two-year-old when the boy had darted out, and when the ambulance came even closer, out of shock, he darted out as well—and if it weren't for that patrolman running out after him into the street, in truth, he would've never been here to have even thought of never being here. He wanted to go, said the suicide's brothers and sisters, and at one point even their mother came by. Sorry? our mother sobbed; I just had a child and here I go taking yours and *you're* sorry? Even so, said the woman, get back behind the wheel, as soon as possible.

Idling now in front of our house, renovated with another family installed and instilled with a fresh start, the firstborn all gussied up with nostalgia is sitting beside me in the sedan. I wish we could go in, don't you? Yet instead of answering him I just ask if the father had ever instilled anything in him. And he gives me a look. The same screwed-up sidelong look the second son had given me at SCI Pine Grove once, right after I had asked about this boy, he was talking about this boy, this transitory cellmate who—after reviewing an ancient infomercial (*in Japan the hand can be used like a knife, but this method doesn't work with a tomato*)—had ordered a special brand of kitchen knives (*the Ginsu can cut a slice of bread you can almost see through*) and subsequently murdered his mother his father his little baby sister—*(but wait, there's more)* he even did the Labrador (*it comes with a matching fork to make carving a pleasure*), and without thinking I had asked about the boy's race. C'mon c'mon, he said, screwing up his face, as if I were a stranger, I'll kill *your* family but I damn sure won't kill *mine*. And then I think about the plaque: glue, like history, is a substance that merely latches objects onto it, not reunite them. Let's go see the second son, I say, and the firstborn just turns away, muttering something about time. You always have some excuse. What do you mean? he says. You never really deal with us, do you? I'm not expecting you to understand, he says; you haven't cut the umbilical. Our brother, I say, has been away for over eight years and you haven't even seen him once. He's out there on the other side of the state, isn't he? He's only thirty minutes away and we should see him. Look, he says, I'm not going to do what you want me to do just because you tell me to do it. Look, I say, *we* have the opportunity to be with him in the same room in over fifteen years, to be with him so that he doesn't have to be behind all that human-proof glass and steel and deal with himself alone—and you're sitting here telling me that you're not going to go because I'm *telling* you to? His hands plead. Look, try to listen, I have to go in a few days, so you can tell him he can call me tomorrow, and I get the impression that he's handling me like a disgruntled customer, like a man who's about to—if he doesn't get his account right—blow his brains out with more reckless hyperbole; I see him being bullied by time, codifying his emotions into multicolored files or just jotting down the whole godless mess onto some make-believe page inside of that cerebral planner, that cabinet of memes where spontaneity is scheduled, and I want to say that he can't call you, that he can only call a home—and he can't do *that* if he can't call collect. But I don't. Shouldn't have to. You don't know rat shit from Rice Crispies, do you? Watch your mouth, he says. He isn't *allowed* any visits in-transit, I say, and then I turn towards the house and say no more.

———————

SOMETIMES, THE FIRSTBORN SAYS, two days ago at the restaurant, I go on an interview just to turn it down, and I'm like aw Jesus. I don't say it but still I'm like aw Jesus, for after walking the director out into the parking lot, after settling the affairs of the estate, this meal—his treat—has to be strictly on the pretense of getting reacquainted. He's giving me pointers now, advising me on etiquette as he conducts a mock interview. He lets it go though when I don't stop eating and starts in on how he does it, how he exceeds people's standards—and I'm like aw fucking Jesus! But he's being interrupted now: this young black girl with her septum pierced by a silver loop skewering a silver ball, the waitress, comes around from time to time to poke that nose into our business, asking *answers* like, I should go back to school, shouldn't I? She isn't nosy, just friendly and a bit bored, for her shift—and perhaps her situation—is slow; and when the firstborn asks why she's so inquisitive—he doesn't ask as much as tells her this—she just smiles like a dumb pumpkin. I'm wrong, I know, but it's the firstborn's fault: the guy's caustic. I love him but he just fucking is. Out of nervousness the coquette becomes loquacious, starts blathering on and on about some idea of becoming something or another that she hasn't quite figured out yet, and then the firstborn smiles: she should have never interrupted his meal; in a second that lower half of his face burns into a memory cell: the lips widened and elongated has pulled around the cylindrical muzzle and up inwardly under the nodes, as the dimpled angles of his desireless mouth bulges forms and furrows and the bossy prominence of his chin boasts the treachery of an elbow. He proposes the loss of her nose adornment, the end of her future, but yes yes, she says, she's just wearing it today because no one's hardly here, and then asks why *he's* here, of all places, no offense—and he losses all pretenses then, states that instead of focusing on his conversation she should be focusing on fetching him another refill of his fountain drink. The pumpkin—insulted of course—just stiffens and backs away. I stop eating. She steps forward and takes away his drink. I'm looking at him; he's preoccupying himself with the sub-sectioning of his second pork chop, the first having been devoured, bigger than the plate it is on; a reddish brown liquid forms. Fascinated by his physiognomy I see a vision: the bridge of his glasses are pushed snuggly against the root of his nose, smug-eyed—but no he has more than one pair of peepers; sweat is coursing down the sides of his three-faced face as his lips' upper centers, pinched and depressed by the philtrums, are giving his mouths the appearance of three slightly smushed lower case Ms; and after he minces his second meal into a million little souls they are all doused with a specialized variety of steak sauce before taking the inaugural bite. He chews slowly evenly, waiting for the bolus to descend before taking another. He's Dante's Dis. Imprisoned proprietor of Cocytus pinned by a table of ice, a solid river of wailing, with those mouths—desperately trying to free him—intermittently perpetuating his imprisonment by the flapping of their lips; yet right now the teeth are too busy masticating the shades of tenants, pulverizing the poor juicy morsels before condemning them with a gulp—yet he'll just be condemning them again once he coughs them up wholly intact. Should you be doing that? Doing what? he says. I nod at his plate. Oh! trust me, little brother; I'm doing fine just fine. They say wine is good for the heart. I don't drink, he says. But Jesus—Don't. All I'm saying there's nothing wrong with a little partaking here and there. But then he asks if I'm affiliated with a faith. No, I grin, but my heart is good. He takes another bite: chews chews swallows waits; another: chews

chews swallows waits, consuming his unsaidness, and then, You can return to the Academy, can't you, with the inheritance and all, but I'm curious (for the question is rhetorical) what were you doing out west? And thinking about the co-sign I may still need on the loan I tell him about the locked-down delinquents the social work the foster care the schools and the homes; I tell him about the art commissions and how I had to find most of the work myself. What am I doing now? Where am I going? He's interviewing me.

The firstborn was an impersonator, a very popular impersonator of a very popular performer, which was probably the last time he had personality. No. I am still the instigator and he is still the impersonator, for he is impersonating his employer today, just as he'll be impersonating his pastor tomorrow: *Only those who live outside of art draw the ultimate consequences; suicide sanctity vice—so many forms of lack of talent.*[23] The waitress returns with his fountain drink refreshed and when she reaches for his glass of water—half full or empty—to fill it, without looking at her, he tells her that he's drinking it. She leaves the glass and straightens, gives him a stiff look, Is everything okay? her voice slightly hurt, and he says everything is everything is, his jaws working the meat. The heel of her hand is placed on her pelvic bone in a perfect counter-posturing pose, but then she swivels on the ball of a foot pushes off and is gone: a customer wants her check. And as if playing a game of chess I lean back and fold my arms; it is touch-a-piece-move-a-piece with the moment on my move, and I know I shouldn't, I may need the loan, but I want so badly to make a bad move: Do you read anything besides *The Book*? Literature? journals? maps? Everything we need to know, he says, is in that Book, including the map: it's not something you read through but throughout your life. If you were born in Nepal, I say, you'd probably be reading the Bhagavad Gita. And leaning back he stops eating to eye me, You know what, little brother, I remember you asking Mother, you were seven I think, you had just watched a commercial—huh, what was it, *reach out and touch someone*—and the next thing we know you're asking to be saved. What happened? I fold my hands on the table: *Cave ab homine unius libri.*[24] And what does that mean? Jesus isn't the only god. Jesus is the only God, that's a fact. Jesus, I say. Yes, Jesus, he says. No, Jesus, you believe that? Eyes fulgurant, he says nothing, yet this game of chess is now a fencing duel. Even I have the potential to do what he did. You would doubt even the doubts, he says. Pyrrho, I parry, Greek philosopher born before Jesus, believed that every object of human knowledge is subject to ambiguity. So you're an apostate now? Which I riposte: Meaning *runaway slave* in Greek. You know a lot, he says, maybe you should learn something. I have, I say. And what would that be? I'm god. And he looks at me as though I just told him I loved his wife. I...am...god (I love your wife). And he can't stand it, his eyes roll and his fork falls, making that disgusted clink, yet after a moment he just inhales and lets out a long measured sigh, And I'm guessing I'm God too, is that right? John 14:12, I recite, *Even the least among you can do all that I have done and even greater.* John 14:16, he says, *And Jesus saith, I am the way the truth and the life; no man comes to the Father but through me.* And I straighten: No one comes *to* themselves unless they go *through* themselves; the truth does not exist in God *and* me, but god *as* me. I Corinthians 6:19, he recites, *Ye are not your own.* I Corinthians 6:19, I concede, *Your body is the temple of God;* Deuteronomy 14:8, *And the swine, because it divideth the hoof yet cheweth not the cud, it is unclean unto you: ye shall not eat of their flesh nor touch their dead carcass.* And then he cocks his head like a green pooch: Huh? wha? you just take what you want and leave the rest. Isn't that what the Christians did—do? Guided by the Holy Hand and for sake of the religion. *God has no religion.*[25] And he's leaning forward: *I will destroy the wisdom of the wise and bring to nothing the understanding of the prudent.* And although this is far from a touché…I fall away anyway. How's Mother? he says, leaning back. Prior my homecoming, after the removal of her brain tumor, he and his wife had offered to bring the mother into their home, or at least until they could confine her to a home, yet she just couldn't condemn herself to that spotless usurpation of space, to that nicely manicured steam-pressed hypocrisy of a life pent-up by tempered imperial love and iron reason without the sweet sweet prescience of a grandchild therein: the baby he'd been trying to beget for years. He wouldn't even *have* that house if it wasn't for the mother—and what about the stairs, where would she sleep? Who would she talk to? He doesn't talk to people he talks at them, and his wife is so submissively under his thumb that you would have to talk to her in her sleep to get her opinion.

How's Mother? he says, solemnly this time. You should see for yourself, I say. I've been meaning to ask you, he says, what happened to your mouth? how did you get that scar on the back of your head?—excuse me. And then he looks around. Where's that waitress—you want something else? And when I don't answer him he just gets up and pays at the counter. I hate his tone. That manner of speaking so proper and condescending that you would think someone rammed a cold metal pole up his butt, just upright and unctuous, a *regimented vertebrate.* That's what the father used to call him, a regimented vertebrate. *I was never one of you; I was never a Christian; I belong to a race that sang at the gallows…I'm an animal; you're making a mistake.*[26] Let it go. Drop it. It's endless anyway. Religion is a secondary school, for you can never go back to a secondary school and you can never argue with a secondary student; no matter what you say or how you say it, in the back of their minds, you are always backstroking through the lake of fire for infinity after being left behind the rush of the rapture. Because they're nothing but a bunch of little illiterates—they are! For when you can't *read* between the lines you'll just end up interpreting everything literally, for when you're void of an imagination *of course* you'll interpret everything literally—but the story of the fall would be utterly *ridiculous* if you interpret it literally! For if the *Three Little Pigs* were boxed and buried in the earth for several hundred centuries, before civilizations were razed, and then dug up like a codex, we'd all be bidding our time in brick buildings and beating up people in sticks-and-straw houses, genuflecting before pigsties and gobbling up garbage—except we already are! To them The Book *is* proof. If you show them a part that's inaccurate or inconsistent with another they'll just turn around and show you a part that's consistent with the inaccuracies and equally inexhaustibly moot—like with the Jews! Who are the true Jews, the darkies or the lights? Who are the chosen few? Like I said: inexhaustibly moot. Growing up I didn't know what a fucking Jew was, everything was just black and white to me, so I know where he's coming from, I know how his little mind works: you would have a better chance of shoving a snowball up a pachyderm's ass than ever getting a *Christian* to concede a point.

The firstborn returns and places an old verdigrisy penny onto a saucer and the saucer at the center of the table. I look up. *Every hundred years,* I say to him, *Jesus of Nazareth meets Jesus of the Christian in a garden among the hills of Lebanon, and they talk long; and each time Jesus of Nazareth goes away saying to Jesus of the Christian: My friend, I fear we shall never never agree.*[27] And then that smile again from him: You are morally tormented. Look, I say, I knew you when you were an impersonator, okay? Would you prefer I said you were *evil* instead? And I rise. If god is everywhere…where can evil exist?

MARE FRIGORIS

SARCASM MAKES YOUR TEETH FALL OUT: when we were acting smart that's what he used to say; or when we were acting stupid: Sarcasm makes you stupid; when we were sick: Sarcasm makes you sick; and when we were broke: Sarcasm makes you get dick. We didn't know what the word meant, not really; we felt it: *to rend the flesh.* So he wasn't too far off, our father, sarcasm *can* make your teeth fall out, because you can imagine what all that rending can lead up to. Last night with the second son only thirty minutes away, after hearing him say this on the other end, I pushed out a chuckle or two, remembering those days of old, the joy I had in my heart the tooth I had in my gap, because when I was on the other side of the country he used to call then too to keep from cracking up: All they had to do was sneeze, he'd say, and the evidence would've been gone; or that his breath was getting so bad it was coming out of his ears: I haven't seen a dentist or an attorney in over two years—ah! I could've made a *sock puppet* that could've defended me better than him. I laughed because I could see the sock puppet. I laughed because I could see all the sock puppets. I laughed because I could see the ventriloquist moving his lips and the tenderness barnacled beneath the underbelly of what he was trying to say, of what he was trying to do, that inner physician, of what he—without cognizance—had laid out for himself; I laughed for I had foreseen his road to Damascus his redemption, I had foreseen all the egotistical tendencies he would forbear and had forbore for sake of brethren inside; I laughed because I could see all the messiahs alive and well today on death row and with their future proponents—their electrocutioners—fingering the golden crosses of their electric chairs on the chains around their necks, and because Judas, according to the gospel of Judas, was the greatest disciple of them all for having fulfilled the prophecy, for having taken up—upon the master's request—the mantle of the greatest traitor; I laughed because the master had laughed at all the other disciples for the interpretations of his teachings; I laughed because aiding and abetting a butterfly from its chrysalis could possibly kill it, and because of that precious beast in my brother in me in *us*—the enthusiasm the goddamn god within; I laughed because the laugh isn't a laugh or a smile or even a scowl: I *laugh* because it is my point of view my prism my power—and the laugh is triumphant! It is the only weapon that wins these wars of contrition when used most imaginatively on yourself. Yet the shadow of my laugher would seem to exacerbate the second son at times and make him feel the butt even more. But you're the one making me laugh, I'd say. Am I killing you or are you killing me? Who's killing whom?

The father did it, the father made us laugh, or maybe it was the Christian academies that did it, those beat-downs of dualism and doom and that white education and disorientation that sometimes befall children suddenly separated and airdropped like Bibles into black public schools—for all the suffering in the world comes from this belief in duality and it started in Sunday school, it started with the devil. But *the loveliest trick of the devil, the second son said, is to persuade you that he does not exist.*[28] But the loveliest trick of the I, I said, is to persuade you that you are not him, for the devil is the belief in duality and the body must obey. Yet during these phone conversations a blinding aluminum voice would wrap up our talks like lunch, yet not before popping up in the middle of when we were saying something important or kind of important or not important at all—but it was *all* important—to drone out some preset address: YOUR PHONE CALL IS FROM A CORRECTIONAL INSTITUTION, AND IT IS SUBJECT TO MONITORING AND RECORDING. But the second son couldn't care less or at least I thought he couldn't because he always kept talking, and when his voice would return I would never have to figure out what he was trying to say because he was always saying the same thing one way or another, as if the father still had him washing the car in the snow or coming in from outside to change the channel: I was the first remote control, he'd say. Yet he would go quiet sometimes, a presence of absence, and there'd be this wall of breath without a ball to bounce off of, so we would just sit up there on our respective ends, doing our dutiful best, until: YOU HAVE ONE MINUTE LEFT; and ultimately: YOU HAVE FIFTEEN SECONDS—

A jolt: not far from the Facility, with white roses in hand, I am waiting for an aunt a recluse, the mother's sixth sister a lookalike, to ready her lungs and legs so that I can help her out of the first sister's minivan and onto this slim one-way street flanked by ramparts of scintillating autos when this man honks me out of my head. Since the recluse is barely ambulatory a cousin, the first sister's third son, is idling the engine before the lowly-looking tabernacle, congesting traffic so that I, having already driven the mother here and escorted her inside, may do likewise for her lookalike. The man honks his horn again. He is a monkey manning a woman's electric razor, a classic incarnadine corvette, and is yelling—but he's right behind us so clearly he can see what we're doing. Against his mother's pull the cousin leaps out from behind the wheel and informs the man the pink-white man that if he honks his horn *one goddamn more time* he's going to rip it out from under his hood and shove it up his ass—and I laugh: the guy's gas will produce the noise like a clown's nose. The man however remains ensconced in second thought; he is drunk but not altogether unintelligent: behind him, here for the memorial service as well, four cars with their metallic laryngeal and diaphragmatic muscles working in conservancy are producing the sound frequencies of big cats, purring to strengthen their bones, so that any vehicular retreat on the man's part would be more than dim. I am wearing a white guayabera for the occasion, righteously aglow in the sunshine, a hot day a humid day, supporting the recluse with one hand while the other is holding a white bouquet, Sir, I softly say, my father just passed away, but if you would like I could give *you* these roses? L-l-look, sssee, A-A-Ah *am* g-getting out. Gazing up at me, beaming idiotically, the recluse leans her weight against my arm and I can feel the juicy jittery flab shaking above her armpit, turning my muscle to mint tea, Yes yes, Auntie; yes, you are. Yet I am thinking that over three hundred pounds of self-impedimenta—the city's bursting with obesity—and a stuttering anomaly can only produce *Ah-Ah-Ahs* and *you-you-yous,* so what do I expect? Ever since her breakdown after her mother's death, ever since her increase in medication, ever since she and her common-law husband and their sons vacated her mother's house (with the exception of her firstborn who's still living there, a premature Oedipus, having had to be a father to his brothers and a husband to his mother before the age of eight) and moved into a dilapidated row house near Fifty-Second Street's El terminal, Let's go for a walk, I say. Let's get some sun rain hail—anything. And she just laughs and laughs and starts *Ah-Ah-Ahing* and *you-you-youing* and I'm like *aw-aw* Jesus just fucking forget about it. (I mean I'm not saying but I'm saying.) She and her sons had lived with her mother their whole lives and their stuff had always crammed these three small upper rooms that were always locked by padlocks, but after they moved into their own place their stuff had already rapidly grown; most of it I can't even describe; it's just this one big amalgamation of crap, a huge hodgepodge of odds and ends, a surplus in public storage—a *garage sale* drastically backfired into an intense drive for more stuff. And whenever she's watching television or foreign films, whenever she's baby-sitting godbabies or sitting alone in her room or in the living room alone with others, whenever she's rearranging the mayhem of her minutes...she cries. We never mention her mother; she won't leave the house if you do. For after losing her suburban position accounting for credit cards, which she had to take a regional train to get to, her overwhelming weight crisis and her ever-worsening condition has greatly delimited her life: her new job now is just to set a foot outside the house.

The mother is going to be as heavy as her soon, for they are both so regularly medicated and manicured that they look like the facades of pharmaceuticals. Annotated prescriptions—a cockamamie pharmacopeia—are always bedside inside these colossal hand baskets because—yes yes—they are going to go to hell in them: plastic tangerine containers with broken-seal promises—for the pharmaceuticals break them once they're opened—and white oblong boxes stickered with neon-orange labels squawk warnings of nostalgia euphoria nausea diarrhea drowsiness forgetfulness aberration to sunlight skin discoloration constipation stuttering loss of libido loss of hair liver damage unusual dreams despondency prophecy arrhythmia dementia shock collapse coma; a stock pile of ammunition to wage war against themselves and ordered by the same doctor they've been contracting for the past twenty-five years to take these soft shells for a shebang of things, for panic attacks back pain knee pain high cholesterol high blood pressure chronic indigestion diabetes glaucoma osteoporotic complications allergies migraines seasonal/perennial depression and for the aforementioned side effects—as well as for the side effects fostered by the side-effect medicines: antidotes for antidotes, and so on and so forth; a war ending with only one death, the only panacea. For complicit in this that doctor had tied them to a bungee cord and—having showed them a Canaan—shoved them off a suspension bridge of belief to then heave themselves up in relief—time and time again—or for however long they can take this gross misadventure of almost-dying-and-almost-living, for like flaccid appendages of propulsion their arms flap and their sex shrivels and their constipation crucifies them—but the memory bouts are just damn-near excruciating to see. For when you do, see them, I mean really see them the clinches, you get this feeling that if someone doesn't stop this soon they are going to go down and never get up—and as I'm seeing this happening, as I'm seeing these wonderful benzo-withdrawing women falling before me, a cool nighttime breeze chisels my face, a homuncular silhouette with an ungodly spherical head flashes before me and I am driving through a dark early morn from a Santa Rosa hospital with a mildly re-tarded white woman on my hands, who walks around at night and feels tired all the time, for her damaged parietal lobe—a stroke—has long robbed her of the ability to dream, to create spatial imagery. She has had a nervous breakdown and took adversely to treatment, so after weeks in the hospital ward I am finally returning her to the home where I sleep as an over-night awake. Another silhouette flits by, shorter this one, some sort of bigheaded animal and I'm saying, Okay okay, this is kind of creepy. Oh, she says, they're just the Peanuts: Charles Shultz used to grow here. Really? I say. Yeah, really, they're cutouts. Wow. You know what, she says, looking ahead, when-ever somebody gives me a pill that's supposed to make me feel better, and then take it away, I feel like Charlie Brown when Lucy, that bitch, would ask him to kick the football and he'd go *oooo no* you'll just move it when I'm about to kick it and I'll go flying and falling flat on my stupid back, and she'd go *oh no I won't* and he'd go *oh yeah you will* and she'd promise and he'd rev and run up and—lo and behold—that *bitch* would move it right when he's about to kick it and he'd go flying and falling flat on his stupid back—God! Good grief.

Inside the lobby of the father's final tabernacle, realizing that this is the first time I have been in a place of worship since the grandmother's committal, when the father and the mother were sharing a bitter memory like two detainees would a lemon pith, I am truly amazed that I'm not busting into flames as I speak to an old devil of a friend; with an usher having relieved me of the recluse, after having taken her disquiets into the bathroom stall with me, the poor man's saloon, after having taken two sups from a private stash I am light-heartedly in the lobby again and presently being greeted by a childhood friend, a bishop of some sort in a blue suit a bright tie and bright blaring wing tips (yellow shoes at a funeral?), as well as a great gold pocket watch and chain like a purveyor of prostitutes, of high-heeled gazelles waiting to gait across the asphalt plains and into the crosshairs of churchmen vying for their affections. The bishop embraces me and then steps back, gratuitously crushing my hand with commiseration, palming a folded bill into it, giving me what he needs more than I: charity. I walk up the center aisle. On the first pew the mother sits with her three sisters in support: the accountant the recluse and the neighbor who never cries; and since the stillborn is ubiquitous five out of the seven sisters are here, with only the other two, the addict and the baby, being absent. I need not look around. I need not rekindle flame for the father's family, for it has been over twenty-five years since I've seen any of these hypocritical apparitions. I just see the firstborn nearest the center aisle, sitting beside the mother, so after extracting a sole white rose for the father I offer her the bouquet, sitting between her and her first sister who's patting my knee now as I stare down the casket, an oarless rowboat laden with magnolia grandifloras and with their legendary scent being nearly impossible to describe. The firstborn slides an arm around the mother and taps my shoulder, and as he's holding the ring from the College of Bible I notice that the Geneva ring is on his right ring finger, opposite his wedding band. I take the ring and take the mother's hand to slide it onto the thickest finger, and then settle back to wait for the penultimate part of the Comedy.

Platitudes platitudes platitudes, grandiosity and grandstanding and nothing but from the father's minister, some peacock whom I happened to scowl at, whom I can't help harping on, sitting here hotly with the liquor burning my belly, for as the closing prayer commences, as I close my eyes to review the movie of the memorial service, the projector rolls: once more the minister has his back to the mourners as he's addressing the other ministers on stage—among them the firstborn's minister—when he intuitively catches my scowl and shouts how alive and full of it he is—the ghost—that he doesn't need any colorless liquor to color himself up—which is nothing more than an allusion to the clear water bottle of watered-down rum I have dangling between my lips when he says it. What a pitiful cunt he is. Yet on the silver screen of my eyelids those Argus eyeballs are in the back of his head, for those bare-branch peduncles are in place of those pretty-eyed feathers. Boy! does he prance. He's embarrassing. He's embarrassing himself and everyone else with the firstborn's minister just sitting up there like a high-yellow pope, amused by it all, enthroned between the other two ministers like three fucking Pharisees, waiting to bore us all to tears with his supplementary anecdotes. It's his turn now, the pope's, explaining away his light-skin completion with that folksy hands-in-the-pocket tone of voice of a city councilman, lauding his *setbacks* in the black church, conveying how the father had found him like an orphan and brought him back to his reverend his brother, how the father spoke with sparks of spit (*Yes sir! yes sir!* the ventriloquized bodies bleat), and how he was a moocher (Good God! how he was a moocher: he'd have a pocket full of bread and ask you for some instead; *Yes sir! yes sir!*)—and my *eyelids* are melting! And—ah yes—here comes the part when the battery-operated microphone is being passed around to collect the testimonials: the father's youngest sister reads her god-awful inspirational poetry from the majorly published book and the only thing more excruciating than sitting through god-awful inspirational poetry is having a public health inspector—not a dentist— scrape the plaque from beneath the gumline—such fucking drivel coming from this drill—and it's an even sharper device at a memorial service seeing that you can't scrape yourself away from the whole affair by leaving your seat; she's torturing us even further with a rendition of a popular love song, and is singing it with such a cracking contralto that, insufferably seated throughout, these *yes-ma'ams-yes-ma'ams* are far greater than those *yes-sirs-yes-sirs*—for we are o-so grateful for the wrap-up. The firstborn brings the microphone to his lips and for a second I expect music to begin and for him to lip-sync, yet instead he just says something so utterly trite that as soon as he says it we forget it. Conversely our godmother, an unpublishable prophet, gets up and says that life without death would be a nightmare, and then eulogizes the father with he was a force— the prince of praise! But then basically calls everyone artless, says that we don't go deep enough, which agitates the peacock who's writhing behind his podium, checking the heart-rate watch worn on the inside of his wrist as though the pulse is timing her. You want to know why Jesus wept? she says. Jesus wept because of your lack of imagination: Even the least among you can do all that I have done and even greater—even the least. And I stand and applaud. The only one. Yet with the congregation drawing such a vast collective breath, in such discomfiture, the peacock has to drown out her diagnosis with a very vocal admonition for time infringement.

When the closing prayer draws to a close I open my eyes and—instead of seeing the white magnolias mounted about the casket—I see the small would-be-yellow school bus re-painted white, pulling aside the sun-bleached awning of the parlor in light precipitation, as though the sum total of the transport's existence, criminal activity aside, equated to a latent retardation. Yesterday while wearing loud yellow coveralls, merely several blocks away from the Facility, the second son returned. Those meshed windows spritzed with mizzle must've darkened his disposition even more so, and as he was looking out of the would-be-yellow school bus another vehicle had pulled up from behind, an *interceptor* with reinforced bumpers and a stall switch to deter an escaping transport. *This* transport is watching the guards, two of them, exiting the bus while leaving him and the driver behind, as the shotgun-toting guard the third hatches from the interceptor, looking east and west, up and around, eagle-eying his environs before conferring with his colleagues; on the sidewalk the second guard halts the east pedestrian traffic while the shotgun-toting guard halts the west, both having placed yellow trestles of DO NOT ENTER on their respective ends. A patroller radioed for an assist arrives. The first guard re-enters the bus and acting as an escort dismounts with the transport who like a tall burly toddler cannot take steps by himself: below the transport's solar plexus there is a small black box conjoining his manacled wrists like two powerfully clasped magnets that not even a plane crash can unlock, while a knee-tapping chain appearing shiny and new, frangible and fake, drops from the box to link the manacles around his ankles—the hummingbirds of a flight risk—with not even enough slack to saunter. The rat-like cry of a seagull spears overhead. A pedestrian with an umbrella unfurled like a checkered aquaterra bird is carrying the leash of her animal along with a balled-up plastic bag, but after seeing a trestle she traverses the street, followed by the stroller-ensconced infant face being pushed apart by the partner who's making faces at it. The Michelin-cheeked bus driver the wheel artist grips the finger contours of his steering wheel, ready to commandeer his vehicle at a moment's notice, as the two officers from the patroller assess the situation by inquiring into the offense. The escort, over-certain in the matter, generates a sorry relay of words and upon hearing the offense the two officers look at one another, and then in front of the transport turn towards the escort: Is that it? All of this for that? And then the scene shifts and these selfsame officers are upturning the twelve chairs, checking their undersides, as the transport aside the escort awaits his entrance like a man under the heat of some clandestine threat, rather than as the threat he is. The director whose chair was upturned first is cordial—can he get them anything? water maybe?—and after his kindness is declined he takes the time to offer his condolences; a bowed spine with drawn-up shoulders and a mitigated voice of gratitude receives his openhanded words, so that feeling like a man now the transport aside the escort can begin his baby steps down the long bright room. Silence is stolen by the sound of the chain, for even with the lights so bright it is still a vulgarity. And the conscience is a sentence even more so, for the deceased is searching *him*, looking for some sharp image of affection as he arrives before the man-size jewel box to be watched from afar: he can only touch him with his lips. He sits. And time seems sterilized underneath this artificial oracle of light. He doesn't show a night. He doesn't show a drop. Yet: Why did you hit me more than him? Their hands, he recalls, his baby brother's and his, were supine, intumescing from leather strikes as outstretched biceps burned like books. Because you wouldn't cry, came the father's reply. A handcuff abrades the knuckle-like ball of bone on his wrist for him to unmake the fist just made: a swept-up pile of trash is before him, abandoned before a kitchen can, and the Sunday-bested father is barking at the baby brother who's talking back and the father is striking him so that now the second son is seeing himself stepping in, positioning a foot and delivering a blow. The father's face ripples. An unassailable hurt. Yet no retaliation, just the hurt look. He's seeing the insides of an ICU now, years from then, he's licking the father's wounds with an apology with self-recrimination, Why didn't you hit me? And the father, pajamaed and drugged, chest laced like a shoe, just sighs, Because you wouldn't cry.

I pass by the little silent prayer hands of the father's clay nose, vignetted by grandifloras, and drop in the bounty of my respect, one last symbol for the trip: an addendum to the book of life in a white bookmarker rose. I also slide into his breast pocket my most recent image and the fifty-dollar bill the bishop gave me, for I do not want him going alone and without lunch money. I reseat myself and check the last entry on the program—and then the mind lashes out: the firstborn has assigned me as a pallbearer without permission, yet not himself, so that now a woman is signaling for me to rise. I shake the noggin no. Once the casket is carried away the first pew is given first dibs at exiting. The cousin who was sitting in the back is already retrieving the minivan, so that after securing the cap on the water bottle, after popping a breath mint, I stand and turn and see the father's brother the reverend—the one who mounted my mother?—looking more dapper and like *their* mother my paternal grandmother, god rest her, than the father ever did— and I remember what the father said he would've done had he graced their father's funeral: I would've cracked that nigger in the jaw. Beside him is his wife, a long forgotten aunt, whose smile puts a smile on my heart—and even the reverend's is less treacherous: *his* smile only stabs me in the back from the front. Outside among these quasi-familiar faces, in this sea of black, I see a fresh white one: a few years ago at SCI Pine Grove the second son had mentored an orphan who was serving a much shorter sentence for homicide, and like several others, by work- ing the law library, had expedited the young man's release due to the expert handling of his legal affairs. Yet if it weren't for this orphan here, a self-starter of a construction business, we would've never had the currency to enable our kin transport from across the state. You must be Matthew. And I shake his hand. He is soft-spoken and handsome and has a kind of kingly quality to him, like a prince in exile, yet after the mother kisses and blesses him he just blushes and ambles away—he will hang himself one day, after the birth of his only son, yet of course I cannot see this. I see the childhood friend though, the bishop, roaring off in one of his athletic automobiles and it is at this moment when I decide I will no longer participate in the rig- marole: although it is solely my wish to have the father reduced to ash I will not be a bystander to it. Not in front of his family. Let alone ever breach the gates of his cemetery. I'm going to see your son, I tell her, ride with your other one. And when she tries to tell me what I already know, that transports aren't al- lowed any visits in-transit, I too am ambling away.

THE SOUTHWARD INTERSTATE, a reoccurring congestion a major artery towards the organ of the airport, is back-to-back today and is still so far away: in the southwest quadrant of this city, amidst the traffic mew on the small connecting bridge stretching towards the interstate, in the late afternoon rush I am granted longer exposure to the yawn-ingesting-gullet-wrangling effluvium of the thousand-acre and three hundred-and-thirty-barrel-per-day crude oil refinery and tank farm along the Schuylkill River's eastern bank; however in my daydreams stands its pretty festooned lights at night, its sulking hot black metal, its glowering towers of orange white-hot of unquenchable quills of flame wreathed in wind-whipped smoke; in the darkened hours of my memory it was and still is a sprawling futuristically medieval metropolis inside of a larger municipal experiment, with its actualized schema having dominated this quadrant for generations and emitting a ceaselessly vaporous pall for generations to come. Several mysterious yellow clouds formed from silica dust had once escaped from an aging catalytic cracker and floated eerily above the roof- and treetops of this southwest section, a community well-acquainted with anemic trees and breathing belched white smoke, and while the sulfur dioxide and the nocuous particles from this oily powder clawed eyes and feathered throats, jellied bones and enthroned sinuses, exfoliated skin while stripping away the linings of lungs high health officials assured the public that no *long-term* perils were posed. Then there's the hydrogen fluoride question, a major component in the complex, a catalyst used to boost the production of high-octane gasoline, one of the most dangerous chemicals known to man used in the petroleum refining process, because the problem with oil refineries is that they tend to blow up from time to time or terrorists may take the notion to taxi explosives or fly Boeings into them for sake of a staggering statement—especially when they're neighboring international airports; in the traffic mew, in this plastic steel capsule, our misfortune is revealed: the iron bird's claw crosses my forehead in shadow like Ash Wednesday, yet like a bottlenose dolphin the fuselage plunges into a tank to breach the bow wave of a chain reaction, the penultimate part of the Comedy: a woman will close her dark chocolate curtains to shield her eyes from her daughter's reflection, a boy will stand atop an armored ice cream truck curing cannabis to be beheaded by a rogue engine fan, the black bear-clawed tires of parked oil behemoths will be wielded to the tarred-and-feathered earth of the wildlife refuge after flawlessly executed somersaults from miles away, and a lethal ground-hugging cloud of gas a silver blanket will creep along at kneecap level, covering five or six miles before dissipating, provided a light breeze or a whiff of the imagination does not carry the plume further; and we will all wither and liquefy like the arugula at the bottom of an unrefrigerated compartment, the vulnerability zone, or sprout visceral beards as Stroehmann's breads do after the twilights of their expiration dates. Reaching behind the seat I produce a sketchbook, so that along the southward highway now, between taps of the acceleration and holds of the brake, I can record these ardent signatures of Armageddon.

The eyes draw out the old man's mangled fury from the whitish eyesore-gray wraith coming from the smokestack. The phoenix is erasing the axis of this city, his revenge is on the horizon, the flame of his retort: *And he cried and said, Father*

Abraham have mercy on me and send Lazarus that he may dip the tip of his finger in water and cool my tongue, for I am tormented in this flame.[29] Enough—too much! For even running away I can't help running away. But I'm stranded here. I can't go back. All I can do is sit here and see these lines of reflecting autos turn into lines of refractory bricks holding the inferno about the body, all I can do is watch the chamber the retort channel the heat of hundreds of gangling conflagrations ranging to temperatures twice the surface heat of Mercury, for I see now not all that will remain will be bone: although the non-natural pacemaker and the hip and knee replacements would have been removed for fear of damaging the grinder's teeth, aside from the basic chemical compounds, there is bound to be commingled in it the melted nuggets of dental fillings and casket affixtures, the mold of a nose—as well as the most unsavory sacrilege: the previous ingredients of others, the leftover stardust. The once-chain-smoking beloved now a six-pound mound of cigarette ash loaded with calcium phosphates and minor minerals will be raked into a tray and poured into a portmanteau-shaped urn, for use as a fertilizer perhaps, or for supplementing the pigments of oil-based paints for that paternal abstract. In any case, with water bottle in hand, I drain the aqueous flame with these alternatives in mind.

South of the city, sitting inside a correctional car lot, I am working on another container of liquor, wondering if the cremation is complete, watching a woman with her six children exiting the building to amble towards a bus stop; the woman, who will be nickel-and-dimed to death, is sifting through her pockets and purse, through correctional vender tokens for transit tokens to return home and then to the workplace or someplace saner altogether: were it night, if the children

weren't in tow, directly behind this newly mushroomed multi-
plex of a prison more profitable than a fast food chain treating inhumanely their meat, she would have the option of ex-
changing her mint tokens for resort tokens, for the recently
opened *racino* along the Industrial Highway and waterfront,
the casino and racetrack. Many mothers gamble here. My
mother gambles here. When she's not merchandising narcotics or playing serendipitous dates she usually hits for some
last-minute reprieve from some lottery, she and her girlfriends,
these three divorced Graces saturated with testosterone-
infuriating pheromones concocted in Korean test tubes, would
plop their packaged masses down in front of golden slots in
dresses as bright as moonsilk to milk machines with plastic
gut buckets and meaninglessly ringed fingers, nails nacreous
or embedded with rhinestones, as superlunary numbers and
shapes effortlessly align in their favor. They are given what
they need mostly, or as much as they believe to be viable, not
much more: like manna from heaven to be eaten for that day
and for that day only. The racino and the lotteries have all supplemented the disability pension at one time or another and
will continue to do so, along with the social security pension
the opiate sales the longstanding lawsuits-turned-settlements
the constant jewelry pawns-and-repurchases and now the construction pension: behind the seat, inside the lottery manual,
death is 769.

SINUS AMORIS

SON OF JULY: you have such bad shakes from a weekly drinking bout that, mustering as much control as you can, shivering
with insomnia in the inferno of sugar you lean over and say
something to this female from the Bohemian region, a Czech
a gypsy who is sitting on the other side of this flange-shaped
bench inside of this colonial square, ferreting for crumbs and
bits of bread inside a sandwich bag for some arbor-residing
rodent, squatting on its haunches as the fluff of its dung-
colored tail curled to touch its head resembles the handle of
a thickly glassed beer mug, overturned. In your mind a red-
tailed hawk swoops down and while she is wondering whether
your whim is under the influence, after a brief discussion on

the importance of being earnest in the feeding of memorable fancies, you ask this woman if she does not terribly mind if you give her a peck on the cheek. She smells of patchouli and tomato soup and isn't terribly good-looking, yet: she has these really soft-looking pair of lips and is so nice and understanding and does not dismantle me—as I am so quick to dismantle her. After removing your glasses on her side of the bench your breath emboldens her with the devil's perfume, as Magritte's *Amants* in their firing-squad-sited head shrouds embrace each other's kisses with concealments: you are pining for a past lover while she—though you don't know it now—is hiding a small marsupial pouch, for she is a mother-in-waiting at her late age and in her early stages of pregnancy; yet as you're rubbing her thigh—god, women and their thighs, my Doorway of No Return my slave ship my center of gravity: if I could climb down this hip as Dante did Dis's to crawl up that voluptuous tower in that inverted hemisphere, on that blessed leg of the trip, I would die a happy nigger. She asks if she can have what you are having and—not knowing any better—you let her have two good swigs of whatever you're having at the time and in no time she's having you back at her place. You find your sensory organ of balance at her place, not in the head but in the giving of such, for the hyena gives birth urinates and comes via the clit—yet with hers having thousands upon thousands of nerve endings exciting thousands upon thousands of more, with over three-fourths of it being hidden from sight, a whole sexual apparatus a wishbone-shaped structure that—once engorged—will embosom the vagina invisibly. You bow your eyes before it. The smell of mother ocean of *mare* of Marie: head being the foremost way she could come, Medusa, so while *severing her head* in proxy, like Perseus awaiting Pegasus, you are wanting her rapture her wings. Your tongue fills her full of blood, licking the vulva the lips, as she honeys the forefinger feeling the roof of her nethermost mouth: the insides of her *cheeks* are smooth and while the tongue is wiggling its laments the finger is *coochie-coochie-cooing* and before long she is surging—forcing the finger out—and sluicing your face—a jolt! Such a transference of fury and pleasure and maddening delight that you open your mouth: tangy sweet and textured light and thin like a wellspring with a bit of mineral earth in it. Her body is floating in a puddle of *piss*, panting, waiting for her ghost in the gown again and when she returns she takes it off and turns you over, so that her uppermost mouth is filling *you* full of blood, but not the blood itself: for after minutes and minutes of this, even after she takes you under the chokecherry tree, squatting on her haunches, you cannot leave you cannot depart you cannot sluice the brown bay of her body the bay of love—so you toss her onto her back and think of fucking Medusa, of losing her in the redwoods, but you can't: you are either too intoxicated or too excited or too depressed or too callous from all the chafing against your mattress, embracing two pillows as a patient would his pills, for the self-inflicted penitent is utterly armored now by a cuirass of tears. She slaps your face and you spit into her mouth, and then you flip her over and have her like a hyena, the pregnant bitch, for now you know now you know, sweating and pulling the silver of her hair working roots while wrestling the shouts of Take your time take your time, *moje láska*—it goes much quicker if you go slower! And then she comes again, a syrupy-textured spume and a sweet sluice cover your cock—and you are connected. You are her child. She has given of her child and now her child is in you. The housecat has run its circles. The mattress is impregnated. The double bed is a doily. But the testicles are a pair of glasses: agony. Yet after the gluelessness of her orgasms, without her endorphins her opiates, she just asks if you could give her fibroids a break and then slips into the gown again: You are hungry, no? And as you're scoffing down slithers of pie slices in bed, naked on a mattress overturned many times, See, she says, pecking you on the check, even a bad pizza is good. Be still. And know that I am the Lord.

I am eating her pussy now—not Medusa's—as I'm departing her thighs the next morning, as I'm masturbating in the cloudburst out back the downpour, as I'm swallowing my semen my seed, peeing, putting on clothes and later at Illuminati as I'm taking them off. But I am imagining those bygone Academy days now because I've decided against it, from going back, from wasting my inheritance like I've wasted my seeds: Henry Ossawa Tanner, Thomas Eakins's protégé, a tall skinny octoroon, the only negro enrolled was only there for two years before becoming an expatriate in Paris: it was said that he had been crucified on Broad Street, tied to his own easel by schoolmates, toting that knapsack of crucifixion in place for pencils to push him progressively darker; and although he wasn't the fiercely independent thinker Eakins was who died underappreciated, leaving behind a legacy of demonstrative oils and discarded loincloths, homoerotic platinotypes and a slew of accusations concerning his alleged bohemian importunities, he went on to become an affluent painter of biblical pastorals and *The Banjo Lesson*—for god knows, being who *he* was, he would've never survived a bright idea. He would've never survived the taste of his own seed in such a society; his crucifixion would've been a mental institution. No, the Academy will not crucify me—not my wilds. Teach me nothing but bad habits. I will become eclectic. Illuminati will become a stepping-stone.

Illuminati: this school of classical realism occupying this fifth floor of offices and studios, not far from the Facility, will either be my elevator to the gods or the gallows, for there is this large open space here with three small stages and models working simultaneously for advanced intermediary and beginning apprenticeships; and with a few of the blinds open to the reliable luminosity of northern light, for it's sunny now, intense gestural and structural training, and a celebrity on the premises certain Academy students come here from time to time to get what they need...and I am no exception. For inasmuch as I detest the ostentatious notice-mes of its founder and director's hyper-realistic portraits, icons of a president a princess a lord and His Holiness (he's a paparazzo not a painter), I am enthused by his mastery of color and tend to gravitate towards his wife, towards his protégé's *alla primas*, the morbidezza of her portraits; and coupled with her managerial abilities and her instructional skills, her inherent self-effacement, it is clear she is the negative space encapsulating her husband and his school. But you can tell she's much more than this. Most of the apprentices here today are like the Buddhists you see at shambhala centers, believing their Lama is special, the most dangerous thought on the planet, because in this oft-heated oft-air-conditioned business seventy-two degrees is the comfort zone. Yet it is also known as *the dead zone.* For after seeing their drawings I have to wonder what are they looking at when they're not looking? And throughout this entire day, although the nudeness is a mirror, after the timer goes off Lu Tao or Tao Lu will shout *Pose...Time...Pose...*and they won't even be able to hold a filament of feeling for who they really are. Time!

I was fixed on a focal point. A bony landmark. The seventh cervical of an adjacent model's nape tattoo of a Celtic mandala. So that now I am shaking off a leg's reverie when Lu Tao or Tao Lu, an Illuminati arranger an advanced student, walks over to me with the whisking sound of nylon from her navy-blue jumpsuit, accompanying the model's fan, to ask if I'm cool enough. Are you sure? It is July and hellish out, but because of the air-conditioning unit it's quite cold in here; yet after having ran to get here on time, after having completed four five-minute *motion* poses for a twenty-minute stint—four stints altogether—under a hot standing lamp with a timer and a *Switch* being my timely cues to change the direction of the pose, after having requested that a fan replace the heater, I am currently sweating between my ass cheeks with a terribly constricted deltoid and a charley horsed hamstring—for I have been throwing an imaginary spear for the past twenty minutes. Are you sure? she asks again. I'm fine I'm fine, I say, and as I'm cracking my back she tells me that after lunch, after a short presentation by the founder and director, I'll be going into the double pose that I do for the second half of the day—but then she points at my penis: Oh, by the way, you're dripping again. I wipe my seeds and sit on stage. I study the activity. In this place these people go about squelching their inner gods, mixing paints and rehashing seminars and techniques espoused by their lord and enslaver the monomyth, because it is eleven thirty in the morning and they are kicking in full swing: on the far end of this room where the northern light shines bright, the steadiest, baseball cap brims are perched above brows for sun glare reduction, stances are precisely arm-lengths away from the magician hats of gray-prepared canvases, and hands are maestroing flowery movements with thumbs and forefingers

pinching the handle tips of long round wands; it is the criti-
cal moment where the right physical incantation of stand oil
and mineral spirits, an odorless paint thinner the colorlessness
of absinthe and anesthesia, is of great concern, and the hour
when the royal manipulation of palettes—the burnt umbers
the raw siennas the permanent roses the alizarin crimsons the
cadmium oranges and the Indian yellows, the viridians and
the ultramarines, the titanium whites and those lazy ivory
blacks—reign supreme. Goldbarth's *1400* comes to mind, a
long river of a free verse lauding the days of when paints and
saints were made with more than just the albumen of eggs, like
with milt or with the creamy lump sum of milk from a nearly
empty human being, with eye makeup and insect wings, with
pestled cherries and barnyard excrement to soften the hearts
of critics, with soils and saps, charcoal and spit, the dregs of
a demijohn and *the anal grease of an otter*—now *that's* what the
Renaissance was made of! And they have the nerve to get upset here about a little bit of drool coming out of my cock. Yet
since I've been posing for them I never knew I had so many
colors colliding and cooling in the cosmic loneliness of my
skin, in such seditious genesis, that a month ago I began eye-
balling an abrasion I had acquired on a forearm: I took mental
note of the blood coagulating *en plein air*, of the scab forming
there and then molting, of the creepy microscopic moles of
melanin speckling and spreading inside out like sunspots until
all the colors of the palette had phased it out—all except one:
that ivory black. They stayed away from that. For skin such as
mine originates every color, and even an absence of color, but
never an absence of light.

Son of July: the Celtic mandala has hemorrhoids. He pre-
fers standing. A daily teaspoon of cayenne pepper in a glass

of water and high fibers fruits vegetables whole grains and echinacea extract keeps the tissue copacetic. Yours however isn't. You put on your clothes your shoes and head towards the elevators; it is lunch and you have only twenty-five minutes left. You feel drained. Not physically but a deeper fatigue: nonconformity is a learning disorder. You can't cork this; you ache all over. You feel like a burn victim whenever somebody blows on you like a cup of soup, because it causes you great pain whenever some cocksucker tells you how talented you are, or when they call you *ambitious:* if a man hears the music and starts to dance I wouldn't call him ambitious, would you? Six years of this though, of scraping by of pounding the pavement while outstanding accounts accumulate, looking for projects to illustrate: imagery-irrelevant advertisements, waste-of-time invention designs, trite commercial plates, tedious architectural renderings, asinine storyboards, corny-ass book covers, cowardly conceived children's books, exemplary exhibits of conservatory beasts, threadbare propaganda printed on Third World tailored T-shirts, sketchy transmogrifications of bipeds at public zoos museums schools saloons, and excruciating portraits from dead photographs for no other reason than nobody wanted to sit still long enough for you to execute them in person have all slowly and insidiously aggravated the hell out of your hemorrhoids. A subterranean dive, just last week, a foreign correspondent from a city paper, a Dane with a crooked nose and a feminine face got all antagonistic with you after charging him twenty bucks for a bar sketch. Twenty? he said, but it only took you twenty minutes. Yes, you said, but it took me twenty years to learn how to do it in twenty minutes, and then you felt really depreciated when you settled for a cocktail to listen to this cocksucker—yes, you're a cocksucker, you wanted to say, and we both know it—thwart any attempt at religious discussion. Come on, my friend, you know the deal, that's one of the two things you don't talk about, that and politics; I mean my grandfather lost his eyesight while watching a lava lamp and my father saw the light while watching a television evangelist—now tell me: who's the blind man? Anyway…you're very talented. Then after quaffing his akvavit in a tulip-shaped glass he proceeded to blather about a lover whom he had long been bereaved of, an author of antinovels, about how he still couldn't sleep on the left side of his face simply for the reason that that had been the angle his lover had broken his nose from. I should write a book about my lovers, he said; they're the most dreadful people on the planet and I've yet to read about them. Yet after a moment, like a silk worm, he proceeded to expound on the pleasures he extracts from sucking predominantly pitch-black cock, said it with these real big dick-sucking lips too—jawns were *blacker* than yours. And you felt even *more* depreciated when you let him extract the pleasure in the car. You can make much more than what you've been making. You can save the inheritance—for even if you went back to the Academy what would be the point? Where would you find the funds for the *next* two years? And could you possibly bear the preceding misfortune of any more last-minute reprieves? You can get your mother out of that place—crawling up stairs and shit, come on. You can get a tie a cubicle and commit for a time, can't you? But then there was that man who rang the Liberty Bell with a hammer and got several months for it. And what about that man who fought the most-sued mascot in sports—that fat furry green fuck with a party favor for a tongue? That attorney a pastime painter can go on to save thousands of homes from imminent foreclosures, yet he will always be known as the man who fistfought a fat furry green fuck and lost: once you put on that suit that tie that remaining thin layer of respectability will be pulled away to expose you for who you really are, and you will find yourself taking a shit between a Vesuvian youth and an aging and shrinking philistine who is bound to be two inches tall someday; you would much rather enroll into a laughing academy and staplegun mattresses across your room than utter those five frightening words every guilt-riddled corkboard of a public service employee seem doomed to blubber while chomping gobs of chewing gum, the universal sign for choking: I'm just doing my job. You lived your entire life without having to say that. That alone is an accomplishment.

Returning to the *Gross Clinic* after lunch there is a live surgery in session—and that's exactly what this place is: it's not an atelier, it's a theatre of surgery. The monomyth is here. That's a good girl, he's saying, that's a good girl. Apparently he popped up towards the end of lunch to rally everyone around an easel to massacre someone's painting with perfection. The poor model the sculptor the double poser I'm posing with should've went out to lunch like the Celtic mandala and I did: she lost a total of seven minutes off her lunch that'll mentally throw her off-kilter. *Get it better or get it worst; no middle ground of compromise;*[30] I've always stressed this, mumbles the monomyth, a short balding somnambulist with an otherworldly falseness to his overtones. The features of his face and the parts of his body would look much better if they were alphabetized from top to bottom, just incongruously slapped together that way in some expressionistic abstract, for being notably indistinctive he remains fantastically boring, as his mouth, the only thing of distinction, a heart-shaped planchette glides monotonously over the Ouija board of his thoughts, picking out decrepit quotes like the dried-up mucus from his tear ducts—only to tranquilize himself even further with his own somniloquence: for we are always under the soapbox of his dream and never the other way around. And when he awakens from this self-imposed séance there would be more of that rheum encrusted in the corners of his eyes and Lu Tao or Tao Lu will have that nylon navy-blue jumpsuit spark fire between her thighs in a drastic effort to race over to it, so that a delicate yellow pinky can affectionately scoop it out, for after telling the model she was *a good girl* for having raised her chin a smidgen I furtively checked the faces of the women in the room, and not one shows either then or now a single sign of repugnance in re-pression, not even his wife's; they simply stare on: mesmerized by the flaccid little wand whisking across the conquered can-vas. Or perhaps their revulsion is much less than their desire to accumulate his skill? Perhaps I've just stepped on a tack of jealousy? Regardless I am the mother of the patient in Eak-ins's *The Gross Clinic,* that grandiose painting that had stirred such a great rouse in 1875, yet is now awaiting the light of day within a poorly lit room inside of a hospital research cen-ter, an alumni hall. Better yet the woman whose painting he's fucking up must feel like throwing *her* hands up in a scream while looking away as he disfigures this poor girl's teats with the extension of bowsprits—the gleam on the bloody thumb of Dr. Gross's hand is nothing compared to the horror of these nipples! Where is the allusion to such allure? Where is the veil of restraint which makes the unseen more visible and wilder to the mind's eye? I feel sorry for this man—I do: if more men knew how to dance there would be less war.

After the founder and director leaves, before removing the glasses for the double pose, I catch Lu Tao or Tao Lu's partial portrayal of me and I am enthused by the image of that half-carven half-crazed ebonized leopard in mid-leap, jutting from the hunk of baobab I brought back from Dakar, from the upside down devil tree of Dakar, where the tourism board had the artists carving them behind desert huts for the currency of cowrie shells and under the iridescent green whips of taskmaster cluster flies and tribal scarifications, where liquescent women—magnificent blue-black specimens, spines erect and regal—carried entire communities on their heads like caryatids, where Wolof men held hands, where the Lebanese didn't mix with the Senegalese on timeless sands nor let them command their ancient cash registers, where urbanization seemed to have happened overnight and the streets were full of lepers begging for skateboards and traffic lights and pilgrims of the Diaspora were squashed to khaki and coin—where the banshee voice of the slain shattered you to stardust and where the driving djembe drums sounded like *heaven* falling down the stairs in crescendo! It's panting this painting, some spur having incited the hams of novelty, half-elusive half-here, tactile and atmospheric, galloping and groping for that which is ever fleeting. At this point the painting could go either way: off the beaten trail or down that overcrowded highway towards a formulaic carbon copy, down that well-paved interstate to an ultra-fine finish where everysinglemotherfuckingthing will be so *realized* that nothing will stand out, because like a bunch of braying brats *everything* will be competing for your attention (for at least with *Movement no. 12* you always knew that the stomach was the star); she will glamorize and apotheosize me into a hyper-glossy double who will look so immaculate that the *crucify hims* are bound to transude from the choristers of my pores. Her painting is at that point where she can still shy away from this. But I know she'll fuck it up. *He'll* make her fuck it up. He makes everyone fuck it up. That's a good girl, he'll say after she's done it too, like he always do, the creepy old bastard, with the same nonchalance he orders his female models to reposition. Push your gift, I want to say. Stop folding your wings to cross someone else's threshold. Our lives are not our own. And we do not have much time together.

But we are bracketed here, the artists *and* the models: the artists by their boundaries and the models by these thin pieces of black tape, parenthesizing the pose on the cushion the stage floor, even on the drapery folds and blankets where the shadowy grace of an embrace is constellated—for with the sculptor the model molded by my arms, cradling her, I am fixing a focal point: one of the waxing crescents at the base of her thumbnail. Across from us the Celtic mandala is setting up for a long pose as well—a sitting one sadly as the piles will pile up—when one of the dilettanti who is truly a jack of all trades and a master of jack jumps up on stage with what *he* feels is the grace of a Degas ballerina to tape the angle of a thumb on a thigh. He has no family no flair no talent, yet he is always in high spirits. And although as a soul artist he may never amount to much, in truth, to stare into him with any kind of pity would be like driving a nail into a pillow.

Son of July: last pose of the day and the moist of her clay is unbearable, the sculptor sculpted by the clay the god the cunt—you can smell it you can feel it, the fervor through these walls the bold-faced lies: a woman taken unawares, a self-birth a squish-squash, like a god kneading a wet clump of clay of itself. And you don't know why you assented to this and you don't know way she's ascending today—yet you *know* why you assented to this and you *know* why she's ascending today: the gypsy is still on your finger like a haint on the head of a pen. It has taken every ounce of jurisdiction to discipline the shakes, but the devil is the belief in duality and the body must obey. Outside the sky has clouded over again and the before-the-rain reigns you in, this impending thing between you two, as the body cradles a body, her thighs inside of your thighs and with the mock of her blood-dimmed lock loosened from the high tide of her twist, slashing the nape of her neck while brushing the breath of your lips—and when you sense the surge of particles and suffer the nervousness of her sex, between the fork of your body and her lower back, you rise above her coccyx like a codex coming from a cave. You wriggle to reposition. That's a good boy, she's saying softly, that's a good boy—or is she really saying this? I may need I may need to, you softly say, I may need to stop, but then you are feeling the finger the slightly moving forefinger of her right hand rubbing your left elbow and she is softly saying to you that she can cover she can cover you—or is this just you?—as though you are wanting to be outside of the body, outside of the office of the body, outside of the shadows and the lights and the looks and the stares…so that you close your eyes. You come. But then you are opening them and you are whispering and shouting and shaking and tearing and she's shoving and shouting and shushing and pushing you—until you are down the hall and in your room, the model's room. You are wiping her back with a blanket, then she is wiping your eyes with a hand, Don't, she smiles, don't: I don't think anyone noticed. And then you are looking at her you're looking at her, the nude being a mirror, for you are seeing his face tomorrow today, a premonition perhaps, like the call before the visit, the visit you will have from him in the dark and in the sleep and then in the eyes wet with joy, wide open: I would've had a dream. I would've had the most expansible dream. I would've been running to the father in the dream and rushing to him and smaller than him—he who was smaller than me—to lay a hand over his heart to ask how's the heart?—and he would've been looking down at me with that smile that smile that indispensible smile to say it's okay it's okay. It's okay.

PALUS SOMNI

THERE IS NO ONE ELSE: someone has to do the errands for her ever-living father, for despite their ever-worsening conditions, other than for bathing or wiping his behind (for he would rather liquidate himself before succumbing to such indignities), his daughters his caretakers, three out of the seven, have to do everything for him; however one has been hospitalized one has been bedridden and one is going witless: someone has to buy the green fan the Chinese backscratcher the on-sale-no-splash bedpan, someone has to buy the groceries and pick up the pills, the diabetes the blood pressure the prostate tablets, someone has to bear the whines and the *wrrrs* and it's not like I don't like going there, to that house to that street, it's just that it has its haunters, those Dantesque tenants who presage the dark paths I could still go down: the grandfather and the twosome of his youngest son and eldest grandson, Stanley and Gregory. No, I don't like going there and I rarely do. I would go for the youngest one who was there, the recluse aunt's eldest son, a full-grown Oedipus now who will be on the brink of a patricide soon; he needs to see and for me to be the apotheosis of my dream, for he was such a beautiful boy once, a beggar now; I remember holding him—all babies are Christs: the massacre of the innocents. Yet ever since Stanley began bathing in his evacuations and appearing around the place in his emetic manifestations (for Gregory's not far behind him in this regard) he moved out a month ago, so until now on the hottest day of the year, as bodies swim boldly throughout the atmosphere in the staunch humidity of mid-August, there has never been any real reason to go—although with Stanley and Gregory it's only fair to say that the antichrist of schizophrenia, that reactionary race-thought of our human tendency, quite often catches them with their pants down. But the grandfather I just don't understand, not why he stays on there, I understand the promise he made to his wife, the promise to watch over the boys, the promise to amass as much guilt as humanly possible for not being a better husband and father and less of a bastard, I understand this…I just don't understand *him:* he has this fish gill on the side of his face.

The street: small cloistered and flanked by houses squished together and rotten to the beams and teeming with super-reproductive human beings, blacks on blacks on blacks. The street: our rites of passage, trial and affection; the street where the brothers and myself and the neighborhood boys would throw rocks at each other in lieu of toys; the street which struck

us prepubescent Apollos with the deadliest of darts, golden
sharp, to race the fastest and fiercest of creatures bitten by
blunted blades of lead, love repellents, long-legged Daphnes
with blurry beads and braids, coarse crowns and ironed curls,
swift boney sprinters who we would chase over broken glass
bits barefooted, that would later rile the wrath of our god-
and grandmothers as they picked out our tiny stupidities with
safety pins purified by the blue eyes of their stoves. The house,
between Forty-Ninth and Fiftieth, is closest to Fiftieth, almost
on the corner, so that although the street is a one-way street
off of the former we would drive onto it from the latter: it was
the wrong way but we had the right. The grandmother is gone
now but it will always be her house, and although this two-
story five-bedroom apartment-house without a basement had
at one time given residence to over a dozen family members at
a time, this house of holiday and thanks, once warm and loving in every respect, has since degenerated into a dilapidated
roach-infested rat-reigned relatively dejected pig sty possessed
by the Housing Authority—yet haunted now by the living: the
grandfather and the twosome of his youngest son and eldest
grandson.

A chthonic gust of musk rushes to meet me: framed in
the doorway is an emaciated man caught so precariously in
the practice of evanescent meditation that even the threadbare tissue-thin coveralls he's wearing, loosely draped over the
shoulders of that coat hanger he calls himself, is also in a state
of becoming progressively imperceptible; I can see the hint
of bones peeking through the worn woven fabric as he would
see me through this screen door if it were closed or one of his
domesticated dealers, for he'll soon blend into the interstices
of park bench slats or subway seats and you won't even know

if the foul rumor you're smelling is yours or not, for like a mendicant child he'll be following you every step of the way, virtually invisibly, for the only time you'll be able see him will be at night and out of the corners of your eyes, standing simultaneously on several city corners, or as you're facing the sun in the bloody tangerine darkness of your closed eyelids, just floating before you in that ghostly jelly like lint. But what do I know? I don't even know why I knock; the door's rarely locked: all the thieves are inside. Hello Stanley. And coughing like a carburetor, sweating like a radiator, he looks me over as though trying to figure out which one I am or replacing me altogether with some mathematical figure. I give him a name. O, hey, I thought you were in prison, and with that miserable nosiness of his he gazes down at the sevearal plastic sacks hanging heavily from my fingers, cutting circulation. Can you carry those? Are there any more in the car? I refuse to give him anymore my voice, for he'll just unravel me, yet knowing full well that I know *he* knows there is, taking the hint, as the custom of aloofness allows him to, Stanley, warped in an upright loom, turns and—like a seed-bearing parachute from a dried-up dandelion flower now a white globular seed head—floats away with those crustaceous toes barely touching the floor, grinning and knowing full well that my blow-off will only waft him so far before he simply returns. The living room, having contained multitudinous cousins and Christmases and curse words of joy, with the exception of certain commemorative obscenities caught high in cobwebs like the distorted fisheye mirrors you see at mini-marts, has been ransacked of remembrances. There is nothing in here save for a taped-up coffee table, a busted lamp with a black-eyed bulb on a de-carpeted floor freckled by blackened bubble gum trampled a thousand times over, an abundance of dust bunnies, and a disconsolate chair where Gregory, slumped in it like a ward of the state, sits with his *state* liquor (for all the liquor stores are called *state stores* since they're owned by the state)—and I am reminded of the last time I saw the insides of my old house, of my last visit there, of the police-raided front door and the father and his iniquitous whores just before I summered in Senegal. The grandfather had expected greatness from his youngest son and his eldest grandson, yet they both turned out to be a couple of ingrates, geniuses and junkies, dust bunnies. He had denied his two eldest daughters a higher education (for only his eldest son had deserved such a choice, although he chose to disappear), yet these very women are the ones whom he calls at all hours of day to tend to their daily demands: to their medicines and medical appointments, to the cashing of their social security their disability and welfare checks, to their shopping and in- cidentals and to bare their domestic complaints. For in truth, though contrariwise he'd love to paint, it is not *he* who is taking care of the boys—or even himself—as much as his daughters are.

Mephistophelean and unseen Stanley, a grandfather him- self, robs his father blind. Every day, sometimes on behavioral antecedents alone, the grandfather accuses him of picking through pad-locked refrigerators and key-locked cabinets and dressers in search of something to eat drink or pawn; and upon hearing of these alleged contraventions you might very well suspect him of being an irreputable smack addict, you might even suspect him of being that disreputable pig who the grandfather caught bathing in the lather of his own excre- ment, just playing around up there in a tub full of his shit, just scrubbing and lacerating the hates and all that they cultivate with agriculture's most adamant diamonds, kernels of corn, but you would never suspect him of being a master mechanic, both affordable and true; and never in your wildest imaginings would you imagine handing over your W-2s to him: for at one time Stanley was such an adept tax accountant himself that, during the launch of his habit (which has lasted over a decade), his street pharmacist had never encountered a single audit in all the years he had utilized his services via laundering rackets. And if it wasn't for Stanley, as shitty as he is now, I would've never been able to motor across this country towards a higher education, for not only did he bid over prices at a municipal auction for unclaimed autos, not only did he win me my ride, but with a minimal fee he had repaired refined and registered that car out of the goodness of his heart. Life's about having the right sticker, my man, and after countless stops and several citations in various indifferent states, in truth, a part of me will always respect Stanley as a flowering aphorist who—every now and then—happens to lay and bathe in the simplicity of his own squalor.

Gregory, the accountant aunt's eldest son, has been sitting in his disconsolate chair twirling the ropey tentacle of a goatee around an index finger when his hands flutter in a kind of frenetic pantomime to an unknown audience, probably to his middle brother. There were four of them once, three boys and a girl, until the second son, a painter and a dabbler in sidereal psychiatry and experimental acid, after experiencing a colorful chain reaction in his brain, an *amor fati*, from the Walt Whitman Bridge leapt into the soup and brine of the Delaware River with the song of himself; and although this happened over two decades ago, out of guilt, Gregory has never really forgiven himself. Gregory was born when their mother was sixteen, so that now he's old enough to be my uncle instead of a cousin and old-looking enough to be my death: he's a walking dead stick, a daddy longlegs with a human head, a skinny perforated bag of bones, a big balding gray-headed dreadlocked-beard-having trout-eyed zombie—but I'll give him this: when he's looking for a fix or a sip he's a regular dynamo: all by himself I have seen him hoist up whole huge-ass refrigerators and freezers and toss them into the behinds of moving trucks as if they were nothing; I've seen him swoop down entire flights of steps with broken pieces of furniture busted-up televisions cracked-up cabinets and a bag of manifold fish, and then unload the same crap with the exact same speed that you would think someone was holding a gun to his head—but the gun has already gone off. Friends may help you move and family may help you move a dead body, but he's better than this: he's a *dead body* helping family to move. On several occasions, with the promise of a forty-ounce, I reanimated a corpse. And he's just a really nice guy, you know; he wouldn't hurt a fly. Unless you want him to move it. Because he's getting up right now—to relieve me of these bags or these flies? Because I've been standing here unanchored in thought and he's just now popping out of his pantomimes. Look at you, he says, all big and what not, and as I'm studying his features, my fingers drain of feeling, I ask him how he's been. Eh, you know, living living, striving and thriving; there's not a spot where God is not—and then giggles under the pressure of this witticism. In the style of Egon Schiele whenever I imagine one of Stanley and Gregory's nudes I run like a boil: I can't draw him; I might be susceptible. I might take a drink. And during withdrawals I can't even go to the goddamn bathroom without seeing monsters in the toilet. But then a lightening bug appears. A will-o'-the-wisp a foolish fire glides onto the porch, and then a gaunt glowing marsh of a man squishes his face against the screen door, with the fatty porous mass of his shnoz all mushed up and oozing through the wiry minutiae, cupping his hands around his face to peer into the dusk of this living room from the early evening amber: Gregory's presence is requested. A seventeen-year locust leaps to the screen door opens it and shoves an amount of currency into the dealer-fiend's hand, without any proof of product to warrant it; quickly he counts it and then turns to Gregory who turns to me with the pupil-fraught eyes of a Kathë Kollwitz litho-print, another mendicant child whose eyes are as big as bowls, so that now with the mounting petulance of a man who is tired of talking a jumper from his preferential bridge (for the jump will never hurt him) I take the opportunity to set down these bags and reclaim my fingers. I *spot* him the remaining amount (I will never see it again), and after the goods are got, after the twilight transaction has taken place between the hot day of a doorstep and the lukewarm night of these foyer tiles, into the bathroom he hastens.

Hearing the *wrrr* of that beastly engine and the racket of a game show therein I knock hard. The volume descends. Wr-rou wrris writ!?! I tell him. He asks again. I shout again. Then there's this annoying interval where I imagine him hoisting himself up from his chair, grunting like an old guard to let in a new prisoner or an old prisoner to let in a new guard and even with the racket I can still hear his testicles rattling like maracas from all the dried-up seeds in them, but when I hear the bolt slide back and see the door not open I give him a few seconds to return to his seat: I know how much he likes to appear relaxed. The grandfather, wearing a sweater pajama bottoms and some socks, sits in his colonic recliner, having bloomed from his anus long ago, next to his only window adjacent the front door—which would've easily announced my arrival if not for that loud-mouthed nightmare he calls an airconditioner, as heavy as an engine and as archaic as him. Regrettably it works remarkably well: with the dial broken off at midnight the room has plummeted into an ice age, completing that year-round sniffle and furnishing him with that forever-glistening pencil-thin mustache, compliments of the ceaselessly running and slightly repulsive sinus issue. In winter the window will be stapled over with thick four-ply plastic sheets as though he is under some kind of quarantine, but today I see him shivering like a Russian toy terrier as he vegetates before *The Price Is Luck* or *Press Your Right,* for he would rather keep his door closed and freeze to death under a satanic air-conditioner than be bothered by the premeditated appearances of Stanley and Gregory, who are always coming in and out of his downstairs bathroom—the upstairs bathroom being broke—to flit past his open door and to unhinge the peace treaty of his stomach with that pirate-cruel mendicancy. After kissing his forehead like a priest I place his bags on the floor and tell him there's more, but then I see the single bed and its compatriot comes traipsing through the door in broken-up metal pieces like a madcap marionette. Wrrru wrret wwry wwredisin? What? *Wrrru wrret wwry wwredisin!*—his drool synchronizing with the air-conditioner's. I'm going to get your medicine from the car, I say, guessing at what he said, and before he can say anything else I turn and am purely shocked to see Stanley, disposed to pillage, floating into the room against its manufactured draft. I never understand a single goddamn thing he says, the grandfather, and that scar on the side of his face scares me, for it's

sickle-shaped like a gill or a meat hook: it starts at the right
corner of his mouth curves downward and then loops back up
just shy of the jawbone to the sideburn; there's even this little
fingernail of flesh at the lowest part of that loop which flips up
ever so slightly whenever he smiles or grits—even more so when
he laughs. You can imagine dirt forming underneath that nail.
It's quite unlikable. Quite unpleasant to look at—but you do:
look at it stare at it; you can't help it; you're hooked. You would
wait for someone to say something that would make him smile
hostile or laugh, or you'd say something that would make him
smile hostile or laugh just so you can see that gill inflate, see the
side of his face gasp for air. You'd call on over your brothers
or your cousins or your play brothers and cousins so that they
too could see, see the old man from the sea, drying on a scar of
land. The scar: the reward of a switchblade. On the deathtape
she talked about it. And it's not just that cut on the side of his
tongue or the dead nerves that's been mutilating his words but
the cut *of* his tongue, the thick southern molasses of his accent
and that lack of education from being black and poor and
unable to finish his lunch in the fifth grade (for he had only
learned how to write his name after the son of his own namesake had died), from being pushed and prodded out by cir-
cumstance and into the woozy world of cotton labor, and then
cast into the sawmill's maelstrom where whorls of grit stuck to
his incisors like fingerprints. A maw of rusty blades might've
taken two of his digits but the gill will grab you, the scar will
seize you, the rewinding voice next: *Daddy got that scar on his face
because he shot a man when he was bootlegging and they put him in jail.
They didn't keep him long but they charged him a dollar and they said that
the dollar they were charging him for was for not killing the coon. Later he
said he was sitting and talking to Mama in the parking lot and the man*

came up and grabbed him and cut him on the face when he was talking to Mama, and that happened just before they got married. He got married when he was fifteen and he had Varnnie Mae when he was sixteen. That's why they used to go out dancing and drinking when she got old enough… Everything that comes out of his mouth comes out with a *wrrr* heralding every single word, and he may look half-man-half-fish but—believe you me—he sounds all Scooby Doo. I love him but he just fucking does. Sometimes you understand him. I mean you do and you don't; it's like being in a house that's been blown apart: you're both on the inside and the outside at the same time. Once I made the mistake of trying to interview him for that blood fable endeavor and whenever I tried to tape him, no matter how many times I rewound that thing to listen closer, he always sounded like he was still going backwards. After his wife died he kept asking me to ask him about himself, to tape him down, but only his daughters can really get him; I have to surmise going by good grace gestures and common mutterings, or just embarrassing him from time to time, I suppose, by asking him to repeat or re-repeat what the hell he just said. I think this is why I don't talk to him too much. I think this is why my brothers and my cousins and my play brothers and cousins don't talk to him too much. We just smile and nod and laugh and give some general universal reply like *alright alright, okay okay, good good, uh-huh uh-huh.* I feel bad. I never really taped him down. I mean it's not like he's dead or anything—as much as he'd like to be: *Daddy's dad left when he was young because he shot a white man who was trying to shoot him. They put him in jail and was going to hang him the next day but the sheriff let him go that night and told him to run away and never come back, to never come back to Georgia and so he went to Florida. Went down and died in Florida, a car accident; he drowned. That's how his daddy died. That's why his daddy left. He couldn't come back because they were after him for killing a white man and he shot the white man over bootlegging because he was a-bootlegging too. So there you have it. Your great grandfather was a bootlegger and a murderer to boot...*

I put away the groceries I set up the green fan I scratch his crusty gray back with the backscratcher, but as I'm recording him in a sketchbook that seventeen-year locust leaps from the downstairs bathroom in a magnificent maneuver of cartwheels. Out of all my blood, those who are accessible, I have yet to draw the grandfather, and he's dying to be put down. So without the earplugs, I forgot them, I try toning out the television for his favorite program is on, a game show: prior to the passing of his love, before the colonic recliner, the grandfather had favored his game show on his makeshift patio; and although that fenced-in asylum aside the house was far from being the slapdash construction he had made at age eighteen, a one-room domicile still standing today with its correlated tin roof rusted and riddled with gargantuan holes, dripping Spanish moss and rainwater into the rusty memory of a metal tub, undulated with water moccasins and lilies, it was *his* patio, made out of necessity and with his own two hands. He and the unemployed and the unemployable would sit under that rug-thatched canopy to take in the view of a parking lot full of broken glass bottles and rats and a Barbadian vendor who would barbeque mystery meat every Sunday from a blackened oil drum, which had been laid sideways blowtorched open and welded to an iron trestle that—till this day—remains immovable. While the grandmother smoked choked cooked cleaned kicked the cat washed sewed babysat and did whatever needed to be done the grandfather would be out there under that rug-thatched canopy, telling anybody who was everybody and anyone who would listen that he was going to go first that he was going to go first that he was going to die before his love— yet despite the arthritis and the price of his luck, every night, he still sleeps with his fingers crossed: *Daddy's mama died of a heart attack when he was young. He got married at fifteen and he must've been nine or eight when it happened. He was raised after that by his sister Bertha and a lady named Ms. Rassley or Ms. Raspby. She raised Mama too, because Mama's mama had died early on. Ms. Rassley—yes, Ms. Rassley, she took care of Daddy and Mama and that's how they met. He always says he wants to die the way his mama died, soft and light and in his sleep…*

Love plagues him: whether fixing him from beyond the back screen door by day as he slaves over burners for two grown men, cooking eggs and grits and slices of Spam, as he spreads around his natural remedies, oil of peppermint for the rats, basil in the cheese bags for the flies, and diatomaceous earth for the bedbugs, or as he clips his toenails on the front porch (the side canopy being dismantled) her long harvest breath singes his nape hairs, bringing back his migraines as well as auguring a life of lingering servitude, Take care of the boys take care of the boys, you promised to take care of the boys. On inflorescent nights when the moon is an open wound, wearing her pink polka-dotted nightie, on cauterized stumps she glides several inches above the blackened pieces of bubble gum to carry upstairs to her boys, barehanded, the big boiling pot of her perspiration, spilling with a swill of rice beans and collar greens as well as the unmanicured hooves of her feet. On the first of the month, in public, she harangues him about the bills and the gambling and the drinking and the copious amounts of cigarettes he orally incinerates, about the bunch of bastards he had out of wedlock, so when he cries and begs for his love to let up even the most abject creature on the street refuses to pass the time with him anymore.

It is during a commercial intermission when he leans over in his chair and clears his throat, but then pauses: over his bifocals I can clearly see his eyes, I'm leaning so close; his skin is as tough as a leather belt and his hair is so fine and thin that it looks like a babe's from all the medication and old age, but somewhere down the line, no one knows when, he has acquired the cerulean rings of an ice planet around his irises— yet they seem to emanate a gaseous aura of spontaneous contempt: he has the blue eyes of a stove. The Antichrist of glaucoma perhaps, the silent thief of sight? Or the antichrist of high cholesterol?—aka, that reactionary race-thought of our human tendency. There are so many misbeliefs, aren't there? So many angles in which to assail the stupidities of perfection, our inborn immaculacy—for disease is a fact but not a truth. I look into his eyes—which will one day turn on him completely—and for whatever reason, as when I stare into those scrawny little legs of his, I feel a tingling sensation in my own: a premonition perhaps, of when my own body will become a crypt for antichrists, a tomb for antigens instead of a hotbed for antibodies. I look into those incendiary eyes and my legs tingle and my eyes twitch and then four dipteral appendages of propulsion are frying before me in a black cast-iron pan, rounding the albumen of a pair of runny and jaundiced eyes— for this is the breakfast lunch dinner, the new so-called diet he's on: two lightly fried eggs, sunny-side up, with the edges light and crispy and thin like the diaphanous wings of a dragonfly. He is pausing now so that I can look into him, and then: Wrri wrrad wrro wrridea, he says, wrrat Wrri wrras wrronna wrriv wrris wrrong. And when he sees that I don't understand, after picking up a plastic cup to expel a greenish gob of sputum into it, he yells, *Wrri wrrad wrro wrridea wrrat Wrri wrras wrronna wrriv wrris wrrong!*

Slower.

Wrri wrrad wrro wrridea…

You had no idea…

Wrrat Wrri wrras wrronna…

That you was gonna…

Wrriv wrris wrrong.

Live this wrong?

Wrro!—wrriv wrris *wrrong.* Wrriv wrris *wrrong.*

Long? Live this long?

Wrreah.

The sister that died, the baby that got burnt up, was Margaret. Her name was Margaret. What happened was her and Uncle Riley was playing and fighting over a book and Uncle Riley took it and set it on fire and put it to her dress and she got burnt up running with her clothes on. She died getting burnt up, that's how she died. They were arguwing over a book. The two other sisters died when they got older; Bertha got breast cancer and she was the oldest, and Ida had asthma and didn't take good care of herselfs. The two brothers died after that; JP, John Paul, died because he just died: old age. And Uncle Riley had an aneurysm over in the woods—drank and instigated stuff all the way through, a little fire-starter until the day he went. So that's it. That's that. Only now there's the baby boy… at the time of the taping his love was alive. He is the only one left. I should have never started this sketch. I should've never looked into the eyes of Thanatos for any kind of answer, no matter how well-hidden the question is—for it is truly like asking a barber if he thinks you need a haircut. I should've never stained the thoughts with blood fables in the first place: after all these years he is nothing more than a soul with cigarette holes. He is going to outlast everyone, just as the second daughter predicts, for he is the one who is making her sick. Methuselah is going to live a long time, she says. A very long time. And my son…he is going to kill me in the process.

OCEANUS PROCELLARUM

THE ROOM IS DEAD, MEDUSA; immured in dilative dark, my darling, I have become transparent; in bed I lie unmade by the migraines by the cluster of brown bats, a bed for she has brought me a bed a twin-sized bed that can't even support my entirety: the feet hang off the edge as boredom, *garra rufa*, nibbles away at the dead cells on my toes. Sleep is the reward of feeling. I am tired of sleeping. I was the dream, Marie, the customary nightmare, I was losing my teeth: masticating I had stopped to test a tooth to wiggle it and wiggle it until—horror of horrors—out came a canine between thumb and forefinger like a calcified drop of semen, an augury anchoring that cantankerous root to my heart, that mandragora which will cry and kill the woman who rips it out; and when I pulled out several more I was eating pudding or soup or sucking on a peach pit in pull-ups, so that now inside of this parody of a body I have become so transparent and obscene as to fall through a wall. I am a dead rat in the wall. Now the room is rank. Yet the downstairs apartment will be available soon: the veteran neighbor is in a chrysalis and to this side of glory he is not expected to return—although the grandson will hold the lease for the two more weeks. After years of taking these steps she will no longer have to; however could this have been the foremost fitness circulating the blood and keeping her vertical? With the ex-husband's construction pension and a good portion of the lastborn and the second son's inheritance (the firstborn being a family man), though she wasn't able to procure a new one, she has ridded herself of the subcompact for a secondhand sedan, satisfied some arrears, met the teenage granddaughter's educational costs, supplemented her medical coverage for medicinal purposes, and purchased a few incidentals for her sons' and her sake, for she is bound to this city for eleven more years until the second son's sentence is up, or until he can be paroled and placed into another place besides this one (ex-convicts being denied public housing), a place that will no doubt come to her as yet another last-minute reprieve. He can take care of her; he can take her weight. And with the few thousand I have left I can continue with the studies, here or elsewhere. It is September, not far from the anniversary of her birth, and if I do not make a decision soon, in the dead of winter, I will surely find myself buried beneath these floorboards in a downstairs apartment.

Comparison is the root of all pain, my love, a suffering choice a schism of the heart: I should've never revisited you—you who never knew. Last winter I should've heeded the warnings of nostalgia, reopened the wound. Out west every palm was a promise of no snow a rainbow, and after years of reliving this city this natal city I feel the way the second son feels about prison and picking up litter along the interstate: once you're inside you should stay inside until you're out for good, no sense in torturing yourself with glimpses of what you already have to forget. The Pacific. I forget it. Making love to you, Medusa, inside the gutted mother of a redwood only to reemerge covered in charcoal from that burnt-out womb. I forget fucking on the edge of an ocean cliff: the tall rippling sea of yellow grass, the marine clamor against your perpendicular spine, and the jangle of your bracelets as you were rolling over me like a breaker, spuming, with the sun shouldering your significance while shining about that buoyant silhouette of kelp curls—or could I have been basking beneath the free-swimming sexual form of a subumbrella, being stung obliviously? I forget not seeing your face of death. All I could see from under your ass was the silhouette of a medusa saying, Someone's coming someone's coming, and then a long guttural sigh, some release by way of my removal of that long yellow screw in your thigh (for rarely did you arrive like this with me inside of you)—for in this upright epilepsy, in this trancelike state, you had pushed away my hands as though I were interfering and when *I* went stiff and hoisted you... I could feel the cool ocean mist as I tasted the saltiness of my sea... I forget the pleasure of crossing the Golden Gate, of taking the longer drive, of how at an intersection in the city of Saint Francis you pointed towards one of the dispossessed seated upon an isle, and I was first struck by the robbery of her teeth, by the jutted register of her mandible, and then by her hands that were clasping something big and furry, wet and black: it had a semi-prehensile tail that nearly snaked a forearm like an opossum's or a cat's, but it was a gargantuan rat's—and she was stroking the beast as it nuzzled her bottom lip; she was crying manically as the rat was *kissing* her, as though it were trying to offer some great comfort during a greater time of torment and I forget asking you, later over the bay, if love was an emotion, and you said that you can't divide the indivisible any more than you can divide the individual—individual, you said, such a tragic misuse of the word: one who is undivided... I forget the necklace of lights wrangling the Lake of Merritt at night, that tidal lagoon over the bridge dividing the bay and that newly constructed cathedral, a fortress of belief a glass vulva refracting the sunlight inside the atrium; I forget the sundry population of aquatic fowls ducking their domes beneath the feather-skinned soup like upside-down periscopes combing for food, the school of waddling geese stopping traffic like a field trip, the meek inheriting the earth without a care or a clue, the great white virgin pelican flying its star-like gourd, the black-crowned night heron balancing upon its solitary stilt, with its spearhead pointing towards the antediluvian inlet of the lake, letting in the estuary, just as indiscriminately as its beady red eyes would wait for a morsel of meat to plop out of the backside of an aluminum-enwrapped Burrito truck. I forget the weird and twisted ground-crawling pines, reclining old ladies in floppy virescent hats, inspiring growth beyond timberlines, the fewer people and the ghost town-tumble weed feeling compared to here, the palm fronds fanning the easy laughter of the blacks, the parched and rainless mouths of the summer months, the blue hills and the verdant terra firma, the cows and the whiff of their coprophagists-covered dung trailing the breeze, the long-mane steeds—the ambassadors of legroom—taking in the deep bucolic gulps of their hair, the highway being miles away and the speed boat, a jet engine, trailing the white frothy wake across the patch of cloudless waters... I forget our star easing into the ocean for that slow-motion submersion, inspiring applause while silencing the hands of a haiku death poet, for he would clearly hear the hiss could the ears be plugged with the gist of it; I forget the chilly summer fog rolling over the steep hills of the city of Saint Francis, a terminal city on the edge of the night of the world it seems when crossing the bay, and whose elite are always absorbed by the fog of their prosperity; I forget the look on the mother's face when she was visiting once, when she saw the city's sewage plant surrounded by blacks and Samoans and the orange nighttime lights of an oil refinery—yet when we stood on a Hunter's Point hill, near that cesspool, even I had to concede its spectacular view; I forget the magnificent Pacific lapping her ankles for the very first time the only time: it took us twenty minutes to cross Stinson sands and another twenty for her to rest upon a wet log, yet as soon as the breath was abated and the pants were rolled up, like a pudgy pelagic bird, she was out there wading into the tongue. And I forget the sorrow of seeing it. She was so free... I forget those everlastingly living redwood groves, those giant sequoias, the largest living things on this rock past or present, those towering Methuselahs indestructibly held up by the strength of their interwoven roots, fused together as they grip fog drip, fog which sometimes crosses the bay only to dissipate before the borders of your city, the Cradle of the Panther: for in times of indecisiveness, when the ground is most fertile, it is very important to not be afraid of being afraid...

We are the stately pelagic birds in the October nest now, my love, a downstairs apartment, flightless with mammoth wingspans and wave-walking ability and within a single week some weeks, despite the Decalogue of color, the ten trees lining the lane and the dash of the red cardinal, under the vagaries of the gods, inside of this amphitheater of a city we will see a tetralogy of seasons—although the snows of yesteryear are near, those holocaust memoirs in the bones: last winter the wind had teeth, trees were on top of trees and roofs were on top of roofs, windshields were stopping stop signs and there were complete whiteouts, highways were walkways, nothing but motors drudging and groaning like a dying species through dark downy streets, and to buttress one's fortitude vitamin D karaoke consuls and dark liquor were highly recommended; it was so cold that I had laughed on an iron park bench for no perceptible purpose (unless it was that man who was found frozen there like a beleaguered tongue) and the moisture from my breath had settled to form a dagger on the eave of my chin (having shaved to be a valet)—which made me think of the only dagger I had to worry about out there out west was in the Northwest with you, when we were soaking up a hot spring in the bubbling nude, bound by snow, with a glass of champagne in my hand, the full moon in the other, and the steam rising underneath the eavesdropping stiletto dripping teardrops over my heart. Yet during that spell in the Northern East, inside of a frosted café, looking at postcards of the Pacific coast was one of the blackest forms of magic I've ever practiced on myself: the shapeshifter couldn't shift shit. I couldn't leave. I couldn't go. I would've had a nervous *breakdown* if I wasn't so broke! And the season—the *seasons*, Marie: you've never been hunted. All my life you've never been hunted. I'm tired of it

I'm tired of it, I listened to this man this pink-white man in a pub, a policeman, I'm tired of hearing it; and I said you're tired of hearing it and I'm tired of living it: that is the only difference between you and I. But now look at what I've become, my dear: divided. Or have I always been divided? A nobody afraid of becoming a nobody. Of committing some irredeemable faux pas all the time. But back out west with you I can work with families again; I can study eclectically away from family. I want to paint what I don't see. I want to be a pair of eyes, nothing more. For after surviving the summer the assault is nothing. I have to disappear. The liver won't make it here. The sea is consuming me.

(O where is the now? where is the now? I sound like a man in a maze. I sound like a man in a mirror, a man who is wedged between two mirrors, looking ahead while looking behind, watching the past and the present recede into a self-existent eternity, a selfish man who keeps to himself, a bull-headed man who spits on his children, a minotaur who fills the flesh with his flesh. I speak it, Marie, to you, though you are not of the scenic dead, the terra incognita, I speak it to you: Where is the now? For the dead and the living can both occupy this river concurrently, this current of communiqué of pulsation and vibration and the past-present continuous ever intertwined—for the birthless can never die: only ceaselessly so. For if we die with our illusions, do we become ghosts? Yet I imagine a race of messiahs still, for we are both the psychic and the mystic inside the pool of one person, an infinite body of water where everything is known and has the potential to be known. For only the dead can raise the living. Only the one who dies to the moment can become the moment, the mystic who is ever-loving, for *it is only when you die that there is love; a mind that is frightened has no love—it has habits it has sympathy, it can force itself to be kind and superficially considerate, but fear breeds sorrow, and sorrow is time as thought.*[31] And so I am raising the living, Marie, you—for I have died and still die since the day I found her dead. Where is the now? where is the now? For it was a sight. A sight to behold. Or did I really find her dead? Yet I have yet to die to the sight of it. I am a thought-form a haint a have-not.)

Everything that has ever happened to me is happening to me now. I am still this thirty-five-year-old man in his newly brought bed with his feet hanging from the edge, drinking on a mattress with his belly bloated, and who is chafing now against his sheets, embracing two pillows as a patient would his pills, looking at the perfect pin-up when I see it feel it the reservoir the river…I arrive. I come. And then I am rushing to her side, soiled with seeds, passing through the windowless interlude of a room to draw back the curtain of shame separating her and the living room from the kitchen stove light with such force that the rod falls down and some guy's found going to town, pounding a piece of meat in mute, with her wine glass on the nightstand her claw over the pudendum and her eyes glinting aquatically: she is on the verge of a stroke. (Although I don't know it.) She looks up at me in her alleged infidelity, at the man who looks like the man, the husband who is the accuser and now the juror with the ayes of a verdict in his eyes: innocent. I turn off the television lower her nightie and sit by her side, but it takes two pills and stoking her hair to calm her to calm her—I can't I can't, she cries, I can't please myself anymore! So I give her the wine grape and tell her to let go to let me, to close her eyes and to think of him. Of *his* hand. And when she does she is falling away and outwards and upwards and when she returns she is feeling him stroking her hair: it is still coarse. Now, I say, now we can move you.

At the hospital she is crying she is crying again; she is okay but she is crying: someone has stolen her shoes. I curse the nurse and roll her into the night, into the cloudburst out back in her chair and her bare feet and load her into the car. Yet at home she just turns on the television again, that ancient animation, chews the gristle before the fat and the fat before the flesh and makes her happiness again like a girl making a braid. I tell her I need to go. I need to go. You need to let me. And she's smiling and saying she's fine she's fine, she has always been fine. You have always been free to leave.

———————

IN THE SECONDHAND SEDAN I drive past the development on the way to the underground bar, for it has ceased to rain, a housing development brimming with blinking blue lights and macabre nights for the tactical cameras to catch, where beside the mural of a macabre writer a literary spirit, an urban legend haunting a nearby house for tourists, begins the tale of a king's dwarf, a cripple and a fool, who had escaped to his freedom after fooling and incinerating the king: *I never knew anyone so keenly alive to a joke as the King was; he seemed to live only for joking; to tell a good story of the joke kind and to tell it well was the surest road to his favor.*[32] But then a clocker comes into play. What do I need? What do you need? I need a woman. And so I continue towards the Italian Market, towards the avenue and the street to where I descend the steps the twelve steps to pass through the glass door and enter the underground bar, passing by the bouncer and chancing upon the attendance of the old Academy rival, the Mescalero Apache—and it is *him* who I am talking to now, Marie, as I'm hiding behind a desperate attempt to try to address the problem, the problem of my departure…

And then the timer the timer, I'm telling the rival, is going off and the nude model, exhausted from his other work, is so startled by it that he jolts up from his nap and starts unbuckling his belt—that's when the preschool teacher comes in and cuts on the lights and here *he* is standing over a sea of helplessly sleeping children with his pants down! The rival considers the joke. I don't know, he says, I think it would be better in first person. It was, I say. And then I knock another double back. A second double shot of rum—but what the hell: it's an occasion. The rival furrows his forehead, You *do* know we're 60 percent water, right? And then a bit peeved that he's questioning my judgment I shout, Enough about me, what about *you* you whore—for the females don't get hairy here when you're out of place. Although the bartender, *Sugar Coat*, just looks and reproaches me with a smile. She has had a soft spot for me for some time, having given me these two double shots of rum gratis. She is an artist herself, an industrial designer who made a cuirass from crystallized sugar and displayed it here until here-comes-there-goes-you-know-who, a dialectical drunk, allegedly broke in and sucked it down to the armature. The Academy is going to ruin you, I warn the rival, financially and artistically. I mean what do they have you doing now, you strumpet—that's Shakespearean for whore—pigmy portraits? Velasquez rip-offs? And as I'm saying this, having took a turn, the rival forever the diplomat, that landless Injun in him, just laughs and tries to blithely abate my simmer with sucky segue: Hey! have you ever seen de Kooning or Bacon at the Met? Hey! have you ever seen my cock dipped in peanut butter?

Christ, he says, can't you be civil? *Opposition is true friendship.*[33]
What? Everything is topical today, I say; imagination has atro-
phied and it's sad because you're better than this, you're better than *me*—but you just don't know who you are! And then
the blood empurples him within: It's not a competition! False
modesty, I tell him, will get him a hug at the most. Christ, he
says, if I were to write a book about you the *pages* would burn
up—and that's just it: it's not about *you!* And then the bouncer's looking back at us. The bartender comes around then and
plants a glass of water in front me, smiling, and then switching
that hand towel of a tail returns to the other side of this rectangular bar, to where a game of trivia persists with two well-
to-do painters of the bourgeois art clinic; her pug, forepaws
crossed, asleep by her feet like a dead molly fish. I take a sip
and the bouncer goes into the bathroom. I set the water aside.
It's not about me, I say, it's about sublimating our pain into art.
Ah-ha! he says, as though catching me in a truth, and you're
so proud of your pain, aren't you? But then there's a blast of
laughter and the trivia trio are just dying after seeing Here-
comes-there-goes-you-know-who, the dialectical drunk, come
stumbling through the glass door only to see his Sugar Coat to
do an about-face and take up the twelve steps again: he wasn't
expecting her here, although this has always been her shift. A
gesture from one of the well-to-doers quells the laughter, Two
wrongs don't make a right, he roars, but three rights sure make
a left! Whatever *that* means. And then another detonation of
mirth. Those two bags of pus, I say, despite the success, are
just like every other louse in this city: becoming smaller and
smaller with small talk, only to acquire the scintillating personalities of their bar stools—and around other *bar stools* they
continue to conduct themselves like the gossipy quadriplegics

you see at beauty parlors, with their noses retroussé under the hairdryer of some deafening polemic. Idiots! A cheap laugh, I shout, is always at your expense!

Midnight and more habitués are stumbling down the twelve steps and into the quagmire of beer specials, into the smoky luminosity of an unnumbered night to buttress themselves with spirits for sake of the imminent workday today, so that now I am watching a lone spirit enter into the place, a beautiful Japanese a yurei a pale porcelain shadow and a model for us once, for the rival has just painted her tonight, and now they're rendezvousing here for a drink. She embraces us *wide-eyeds* warmly: last year we had drawn and quartered her nude several times together and painted her twice in a blue kimono with lily prints, girded by a pink sash, yet every time she sat for us, like lust in the treetops, a part of her would always seem to sway just a little bit more out of reach—and then within again in a causal billow of back-and-forth that constantly kept us in a contemplative swoon. Afterwards when she came out with us for a drink, a little ritual we had, in light of the candles we had boosted from other booths, we would praise the promise of shadow, that atomic gloom phosphorescing the pale translucency of her skin from the lucid ancestral insides of her forearms, as though it were the smoky luster of some eighteen-century laquerware lit up by the candlelight inside the semidarkness of a Nagasaki tearoom—unlike under that loud electric marching band we had beaming down onto the model's stage. Flecks of sweat or shower would glimmer like gold inlay, as only candlelight can elicit, leaving her partly hidden and sublime, subdued, preoccupied skin knowing the subtlety of shade, a haiku death poem. Forever the diplomat the rival changes his tone, and he, a man of my many years and a one-woman man the entirety of his existence, having had his hymen ripped asunder by the ravages of a much older woman, compliments the model on her appearance in such a pent-up repressed sort of way that can I imagine them one day with a death erection under a dead tree screaming with cicadas and with their bush bouncing up and down like an overjoyed imp. For after the rival moves a seat down from me, so between us she can sit, they decide a booth would be best, with a candle between the two of them and me in a seperate chair: I am a third leg where there need only to be one. After a few moments, the rival gibes me with a past critique, and I curse him with a finger. I am feeling my third double now as he, working on his second beer, unnervingly chuckles and tries to blithely engage our friend in a tête-à-tête, for she too is fidgeting in her seat, smiling impenetrably. She changes the subject then by telling me that with my long satyric beard and my studious glasses I look like a Moslem, that she didn't know that I was a Moslem. Are Moslems supposed to depict the body? And as I'm sure she's referring to their fear of formulating an idol—as the Christians did with Jesus and the Buddhists did with Gautama (which was why Mohammad was barely depicted)—I tell her that I'm not a Moslem, and that I don't really care about joining another club with my label gun only to have to assume a whole new slew of sacraments. I'm tired of labeling shit. I'm tried of humanizing a god with my shortcomings—proof that I pissed the prophet into a pot! For how can you understand the infinite with finite means? How can you know the truth when to *know it* would be proof that you don't *understand it*? Yet the yurei is making a sorry attempt now at regaining the reigns, a toast, To our art then? And in the smoke-filled atmosphere, with her glass highly raised, she is displaying one of her eczematous hands, contrasting the pale porcelain transparency of her body—yet the memory of the tall black sweet seagrass of her sex gives it a mystique: as though she is really hag whose hands had only repelled their spell. I find myself returning to the rival, his gibe resounds, the same vitriol he had said a month before concerning a semiabstract portrait of myself, my first painting since the Academy: You've been beating yourself up for faction of a second of an image, he said. Which doesn't sound like much. But what made it so vitriolic was that he said it while looking at it via the right side view, as though he could only ascertain the true travesty of my persona from an anamorphic perspective, as though only that particular tilt could reconstitute the skewed skull of Holbein's *The Ambassadors*[34] while saying to me remember to die to your day.

THE SUN IS TOO SUNNY. The head hurts the body aches. I am walking towards the underground bar again, a mile away. It is afternoon and the street a commercial street is sure to be busy, so there is bound to be a parking ticket waving hello to me from a windshield. On the way out of headquarters, after overhearing an officer say to a woman wearing a hijab that he couldn't disclose any information to her in order to protect the rights of the prisoner, I spat into a wastebasket—yet before dawn in the minaret of our lower cell the prostrate mark on the muezzin's forehead had humbled me, as he, wearing highwaters for fear of hellfire, roostered the call for prayer. I'll have to wait a couple of months for the court hearing, provided it's no longer postponed—not to mention the time it will take once I'm found guilty to complete the detention or the community service, where I'll be placing diapers over ovulating twelve-year-olds and compliments over their psychosomatic syndromes. I can't leave I can't go—I can't even remember what I have done! All I know is that I was multiply charged with misdemeanors, that the glass on the bar door was broken, that my eyes are puffy and that the glasses are cracked: I'm not going to hit back, I don't remember saying that, before egging the bouncer to hit me. I was humiliated. I remember that. I was handcuffed and thrown into the itinerant dungeon of a paddy wagon (Now *that's* racist, a judge had said to me once, some crusty old mick, said it in a courtroom full of court officials and cops chomping gobs of chewing gum, the universal sign for choking, right after hearing me refer to a police van so offensively—which is sad because I *liked* the Irish before they came over here: no one wants to be the nigger over here; I should've said to that court that *you people are all covert niggers, maniacs savages misers...Judge, you're a nigger,*[35] but I'm more afraid for us who are being disproportionately placed into these vans, your honor sir, than what they are so offensively referred as—and I should've said it through a *sock puppet* just to prove another point: that no matter how insane I was I was sure to receive an unfair shake), and on the way to headquarters, as I was waiting to be thrown down into a dirty-ass basement with neither a bottle nor a belt to hold me up, where I would have to eat white bread and processed cheese for twelve hours, where every time I would unscrew a water bottle there would be the insane ravings of an inebriated white boy inside, where he would stick and twist a cold cork screw into my intestines every time he asks for the time of day or the phone call, where the television-induced jubilation of the guards would trickle over our foreheads like piss, where the plastic pieces of a sandwich bag would be wrapped around bread ends for earplugs, where every position I could possibly imagine would be equally insufferable, and where I would decipher the cacography of vulgar hieroglyphs before morning, before the sum of these sufferings would transmogrify me into an oozing blob of apology, in that *paddy wagon* I did the only thing that I could do: with the double-jointed shoulders of a shapeshifter, handcuffed, from behind my back I brought my hands over my head to retrieve the remaining rum shot in my pocket. The poison that pushed me over. A trick the father, god rests him, would've wished he could've done to solve the conundrum of a noose.

I return home with the secondhand sedan and from the back door enter into the bedroom of the downstairs apartment, the same layout as above, to find as I have left it the front bedroom door shut—and it's strange, Marie, for whenever I'm gone she usually opens it to make the place seem bigger. Never have I been so happy to be in this room. I put on an older pair of glasses and open the door to move towards the bathroom. I take painkillers and anti-inflammatories, a shower, but when I come out I see what I didn't see at first: the crumpled curtain on the kitchen floor. I replaced it last night. Yet when I cross the floor I see why it's down there again: she is lying abed in her unholy waters with the smell and the heat and the cockroach crawling across the body. I swipe it away and call for her, her eyes are in the back of her head, shaking the chilblained body beached by a wave, harder and harder until a hand goes up like a bid for a life it rather likes. I shout for her. I slap her face and her eyes to roll back into place. Oh God it hurts! What hurts what hurts? *It hurts it hurts it hurts!*—and so I reach for the nightstand to call the paramedics. I retrieve the small black pouch then with the meter and the pen-like device, along with the syringe the vial and the alcohol swabs, yet when I go for a finger she just wails and waves me away. I grab it swab it and prick it with the pen, but then the blood is smeared and I've got to give it another go; this time she is pricked so lightning-quick that I must milk the speck of blood to be sampled: 40 the glucose meter reads. It should be reading between 80 and 120, and so I siphon the insulin from the vial with the syringe.

After the paramedics arrive she comes around and we slide her onto the dry side of the bed. They take her vitals and then they take me aside. I should've waited, they're saying; she's alright, but I could've easily given her too much and sent her off. Watch her closely, they say, for the next twelve hours; give her another opiate if she needs it. They really want to take her in for observation but she won't let them, someone is stealing her shoes, and after they leave us she tells me what really happened: she was touching herself again when she started to have another stroke. She got up and made it to the curtain but fell back into the bed. She was paralyzed and she couldn't even call me, or our neighbor her sister for that matter, so she drifted: missing breakfast lunch medication, causing the blood sugar to plummet—and by the time the paralysis left her legs she was too weak to move. Had they kept me encaged a little while longer, had I taken a longer shower, as when she was driving she might've floated off towards that star-spangled comatose state, towards that ultra-huge half-aqueous lung called ubiquity.

After I wipe her down dress feed and medicate her, after I strip and wipe down the mattress, placing a towel over the stain and replacing the sheets (having rolled her onto her sides to do so), after I dress feed and medicate myself I lie down beside her—and I am tearing, Marie, for our favorite program is on: There's nothing like animation before a film, she says, the tablets taking hold, and then out of some association with the illusion of movement she tells me of the first time, the gang leader the boyfriend, like someone ripping her insides out, of when she first bled and how her mother wouldn't let her go over the wall with the boys anymore, of how her body had come alive very early and of the white hand inside her pocket, of the boys who were her friends and had tried to rape her, of how she beat them harder, yes, harder than they beat themselves and as she drifts further back, by the time she is in the red clay ditch she is fast asleep—and I am seeing what I cannot really see: is she falling down a staircase or in the tub or in the middle of the street and I'm not there? am I *seeing* her falling down a staircase or in the tub or in the middle of the street? am I going blind? am I being misunderstood? am I pissing on myself? am I married am imprisoned am I employed? am I becoming the child and not the dream? am I destroying myself my work? am I killing someone? am I dying in a room full of people who are afraid to touch me…?

As the sun descends I see now not all of our quality time will be spent during the day, there will be quality nights as well: from birth to my fourth year I will sleep by her side, yet from my fourth to my seventh her bed will become a privilege. For whenever the man is home, for the child fathers the man, I will grapple almost nightly with bed sheets as though battling apparitions, and whenever the lights are left on, at breakfast table with spear in hand, fiercely will he rise up the issue of the electric bills. But there will be many stormy nights when she will let me sneak abed under the extenuation of fear, and never will she stir although lightly will she sleep: she will feign sleep until I fall asleep and follow suit, waking me only to crawl away before the man rises. There will even be nights when she will go to bed unclothed to wait for the little thief, for her sadness would have metastasized and she will confide in me; on such turbulent nights under the guise of subterfuge, aside the man who sleeps like a rock under sea, under the touch of an antenna her little cockroach, she will allow me admittance into the wonderful creases of her being. All except one. For when I'll try to quest this only then will she moan and stir, only then will I surcease. Pray for storms. For on one night when I am seven she will be in remission, and several of those antennas will glide several times inside that awful region as agents of pollination to return an eternity later, radiant and redolent of the magnolias once whiffed in the American South.

MARE COGNITUM

BECAUSE HER BODY IS RISING AND FALLING BESIDE MINE, Marie: in the wintry heat of her downstairs apartment, under the hospitality of her bedspread, I lie unmade, awakened by dream or rather undreamed by a labyrinthine dream, listening for some inhabitant overhead, for some little footstep forsaken; I can scan the dark ceiling the ultrasound for the sign of an inhabitant but I cannot find the mark of our little girl's labia, yours and mine, only the presence of an absence we both embosom, Andromaque and I: for after the February murder of her half-brother, within a week, her sister-in-law and toddler nephew had migrated away and since then the upstairs tenant, so that now we are sharing our grievances, Andromaque and I, like we're sharing this flat sheet—and there are way too many people in this bed. A calf drapes the bone of my shin and I can't see how we can stay here; the duplex was in her brother's name, god rests him, but I'm sure she can summon someone else to oversee it. She hasn't painted since nor has the inclination to, and I just spent the best part of the night digging a garlic clove from out of her cunt. She *may* have given me a minor virus, my love, the warts, but I know I will give her something much worse: my heart—and that mandragora she is sure to uproot: my will; it will cry and kill her when she tears it out, my darling, as you always did, only to grow back to kill her again and again and so I had to get down there on my knees and burrow for that garlic clove out of a sheer sense of shame, for that little turtle of a girl lying abed on her back, tipsy from absinthe and with her legs spread apart, a hand mirror in one hand, her fingers clenched in a fist, with two of her other fingers splaying her lips: an upside-down V. I had to get down there with the smell furrowing her nose as the tears flowed from the idée fixe of an even yeastier infection; I had to get down there lend a hand and ream her out, tonguing her pearl to reduce the pain until I succeeded: since October, it is December, in some essential way we help each other through these vicissitudes of life.

I was in a room. A white room. A tabula rasa of some kind in concrete form. No windows no door, nothing save for my-self. No cloth yet I was warm. No light yet I saw. But I couldn't get out: it was like an asylum's cell. There were no slats no vents no visible sign of circulation, but I was breathing—even so, although I was neither thirsty nor hungry, I had no idea how to sustain myself. Yet after making water in a corner I had fallen asleep in another and when I awoke there was a feast where my water had been. After eating I felt tired and dreamt within the dream of the being before the fall, before that mandragora split twins, Adameve, the objective and the subjective in perfect balance—yet when I awoke I was still in the room. Out of folly I drove my head into a wall, rendering myself unconscious, so that I could beseech that self-existent being that epicene to awaken me beside a counterpart, in a bed and under a bedspread, some Mesopotamian fig leaf if you will, some cloth to cover the consciousness up and when I awoke I was no longer in the room. Yet as I was describing my custody to my counterpart, how I came be released, she interposed the opposite: Are you sure? And my lip fell to brooding: I mustn't fall asleep, I said. And then I awoke.

Outside: tiny descending skeletons of snow. There has never been a human being with the same genetic code. There will never be a human being with the same genetic code. In the eleventh week, my sweet, our baby had fingerprints. By the twelfth it had fingernails and its gender could be determined; it could swallow and its kidneys could produce: agony. Days before the procedure you had inserted several sticks of seaweed inside to force the cervix open. The actual procedure took only ten to twenty minutes but we were there for three hours: paperwork and blood work, an inch of urine, ultrasound—she was the girl—counseling options and birth control, expectation of the procedure in the second trimester, informed consent. While you were in the room they made me watch a film by clasping my eyelids open to my brows with the Kelly clamps of several cups of coffee (sorrow's a somnolent, a way to speak to the soul asleep), as the body was delivered in breech position. Everything but the head. The body was moving. Everything but the head. The fingers were little and clasped, the feet were kicking, and the doctor took a pair of scissors and inserted them inside the base of the skull—the arms flinched. A startled reaction. Like a person does dozing in a seat when she feels she's about to fall. The scissors were opened and a power-suck was inserted—I can hear the machine—and then the brains were slushed in like sherbet in reverse, causing the skull and the face to collapse like a discarded mask. The body was limp. Her face, you said, after the year had past, they didn't deliver her face because it was just a few inches short of citizenship. They even showed me faces of women who weren't white…as though only women who weren't white…they showed me five drawings… So that after your next lunar revolution, your blood moon, after being in a hospital ward full of bloody girls watching romantic movies in nightgowns in bloody chairs, feeling bizarrely intimate and yet calling security twice, alone in your apartment (If you stay, you had said to me, I will never be as strong as I am now) you toiled over a golliwog between heavy flows, misplaced passion everywhere, a gnarled armature with limbs curled in on itself and fleshed out with charred melted strips of brown leather; it had a zipper for dentition, two dark vacuous pockets for eye sockets, and a concave chest cavity cradling a leather-bound book resting upon a spine constructed of tiny metallic binder clamps: the art of the book's cover protruded a smooth leather ribcage and inside, entitled *Viscera*, unfolded in length the intestinal doubled-sided hand-engraved hand-printed crimson-script pages of low-spirited prose and abdominal organs, like the primrose bellows of an accordion—yet playing the dying throes of a pipe organ with the yellowing whine decaying the longer the pages were held. I was so taken by this morose piece of work that I had begged to hold it in the keep of my lonesome apartment, and there I had placed it in a corner enclosed by sage candles and candies until I had to return it. But I didn't expect that murmur though, when I brought it out. The way I held it in my arms, crossing that street, made my body convulse.

My contradictions are closing in on me. Andromaque is sleeping. Her rear nudges me: she must be dreaming. I was once told that a white room represents marriage, some people panic some people paint it—but then there's that black-and-white girl now; she was slow or at least she looked slow and behaved slowly. On the anniversary of my birth, just last week, on the day of the sun I was haunting a used bookshop, a museum mummified by cloths of cat hair, leafing through a sheaf of contemporary prints when out of the corner of my eye I noticed this little girl standing by: her gaze had manifested me from myth to man, for everyday like a thought-form a haint a have-not you never really exist until a child says hello to you. Yet I was apprehensive about returning her look for her grandmother or who looked to be her grandmother, a pink-white woman with a pomp, was closing in on us and without saying a word was already leading her outside by the hand, but as they were crossing the intersection into the chilly afternoon light, no longer hand in hand, I pretended to wait for a trolley. The grandmother was already across the street when the girl had stopped turned and stooped halfway, as though looking for something she had dropped—yet froze there. Examining the street in the middle of the street. Until she realized she was being abandoned and stumbled after the grandmother.

My eyes, Marie. I don't restrain it. Andromaque curls herself into me. Her body softens me. I wipe my eyes and reach over to tuck the flat sheet beneath her unexposed flank: there is a jingle from the indoor wind chime; it reminds me of you and your bracelets and of the ties that bind—has your love fallen afoul of mine? Yet with optical aids I can clearly see the zodiacal wheeling of the nightclock; light pretty soon will be prying back the curtains, peeling walls of drabness with color for the construction of a new day. Andromaque turns and gives me her back; it yawns and glows in the dark. I replace the glasses on the nightstand and ease a hand around her now-exposed flank, placing kisses between her shoulder blades as the fingertip is working meticulously. She moans. Her spine flattens for me to slide towards her center her scent, for me to pretend I am her last month in the bar, tonguing the webbing between my thumb and forefinger to show me how she likes it, and I lap up that absinthe garlic and blood: an act of worship inasmuch as I can taste our own transubstantiations: at first we couple and crawl like a nightcrawler underneath a gigantic thunderclap, apocalyptically slow with our spoor washing away in the waters and with every inch of us on tenterhooks, bearing the weight of some imminent threat, of some deep squishy intermolecular hurt, and then we're galloping off like a fire giraffe with the arms of our maw wide open, slicing through the clouds of ripe fantasies and fleshy afternoon dates, only to end spooning as two sentries would in a wintry outpost, exposed to the solar element, snowblinded and numb and licking each other for a taste of what's to come. I want to leave this city. I like this city. Dear heart, which part? And our voices are so soft you could crush them with light—although the dialogue is loaded like a die—and when she faces me Cupid's bow could be the crest of her upper lip, for she is tetanizing me with a kiss: *A city becomes the world,* she says, *when one loves one of its inhabitants;*[36] happiness is the shadow cast by the light of the moon, my love; the woman who gave you life could move into the downstairs apartment of the woman who could give you a life; you and I could move upstairs, despite the spirit up there—our love can act as a charm…yet you're smiling, aren't you? My face must be blank for she's inserting my answer. Just as a fist releases a fly out of shock, so too does a great beauty capture you—yet even a greater beauty frees you from itself? O, dear heart, which part?

Under the showerhead I sulk, as a nude model I bare all; I have a cargo of commitments, various engagements since I've dwindled the inheritance: one more weekend with a group of girl scouts who'll probably sing around me like a campfire again and a couple of one-month poses, one at the Schuylkill Studio every other weekday (for they're either sculpting my skull or delivering it, using calipers as forceps to measure my dimensions) and a six-hour stint at Studio Illuminati every other weekday in between; I even show a private viewing of the body once a week to a woman who breastfeeds in front of me—although this is the only honor. I need to sequester myself; I'm snowed under. The city necessitates the solitudes. I haven't had time to create; I have all the violence of the stars and yet I cannot chart the *shifts*. Call Schuylkill, I say to myself, tell them why you didn't come in yesterday and decide whether you should go into Illuminati today—because it's eight and you're supposed to be there by eight. Yet even if Andromaque drives you you are across town and—before nine—you will never make it. After that outburst way back they didn't call you for a month. But so what. I mean they can color their asses off but they can go to hell. Fucking Nazis the way they make you stand up there all butt-naked and cold with them little-ass heaters they got—it's *freezing* for Christ's sake! Someone should open them damn blinds and spread some of that natural northern light onto y'all dim wits, because y'all always got the nerve to look at me all funny when I ask for a fan—can *I* help it if I have to run through thirty blocks of anger and snow just to get here on time? Not to mention, from the get go, y'all always got me doing these stupid-ass motion poses just because I can stand taking it on one leg while throwing an imaginary javelin like a *mother*—portrait of a spearchucker, that's what I call it! Just give me a damn fan and don't be looking at me all funny when I ask for it. Winter or no winter. That's all I ask.

La-la-la, feeling a bit better now I step out the shower, la-la-la, stand and drip before the mirror, yet it is gripped by fog drip so I move into the kitchen and look into the cabinets. I go into the bedroom: Andromaque is asleep; she's a downtown bartender. I return to the kitchen and stoop beneath the sink to remove the muscatel; it was behind the bleach. However: if not Schuylkill, I say to myself, call Illuminati at least; you need the money—and then there's that *model* there today! But as I'm imagining lying abed with her again, going on and on about her terrible son, I say I *am* your son—and call out. But they're like *whoa whoa whoa* you don't need to call out, you don't need to come in; we've replaced you; and I'm like wha? and they're like yeah and I'm like who?—like it's any of my business—and they say this dancer dude, just called him up and he came right over and blah blah blah. Well, there was no blah-blah-blah on their part really, because after I blathered something about being sorry or sick or dejected they just hung up. Beforehand though I was quick enough to say that I am *definitely* free next month and most of next year and *blah blah blah*; I've been calling out a lot lately—and it's not because of the migraines either. I quaff the wine I've poured. I hate that though. I hate it when someone says that they don't need you when you're thinking they need you—as if you can leave as if you can go. I've been posing for them since the summer and they haven't even offered me a discount yet; bartering modeling time for studio time isn't a discount, that doesn't count—not at all! We *may* be able to help. But I bet the red man didn't have a word like that in his repertoire until the Mayflower came. Such a wishy-washy word. You *may* have it or you *may* not. May: the goddamn genital wart of the English language. Life could very well be *a sexually transmitted disease*, if Laing is right, and the mortality rate could be a hundred percent, if these vicissitudes are not cathartic and shamanic in nature.

———————————

PRISON IS A BETTER PLACE, the television tells me, for on State Road, a warren of weigh stations of jails not a prison, the second son was less prosperous. Since Illuminati has replaced me I am free to take the mother's place for virtual visitation, for her left knee is oppressive; I have taken a regional train from outside of the city to the center of the city to walk towards the Society, addled by muscatel, to hear the television promote more freedom in prison, more privileges, only two to a room, more options and better classes, plenty of time to study and genuflect without the fret of debt. I listen to it intently, because sometimes I fantasize: maybe I'll learn to be a good little conduit, maybe I'll create some unexampled masterpiece by pulling a rabbit out of my ass and having it luxuriate in tertiary tones, or maybe I'll just burn a book into their souls instead— maybe I'll feel the way about my words the way Baldwin felt about his: *I love writing so much that when I die I want to die in the middle of a sentence.* Yes, maybe I'll just crawl on out of my foxhole because I'm tired of staying free. If I cannot satisfy the wanderlust, if I cannot make my way towards the solitudes *to lurk in crystalline thought like the trout under verdurous banks, where stray mankind should only see my bubble come to the surface*,[37] then I shall stroll straight in there and mark my fear off the calendar—for like a stray, sooner or later, after a godless fuck I'm going to get hit. I'm going to get up and go right out into traffic and get run-ed-ed over really nice and good.

But State Road is an intermediate state where little or no privileges are to be had or gained, where you and all of the other complaints are packed into an overcrowded holding cell to feed off of each another, where you storm into a compound of storms: the manifold glut of gripes from sodomites and rapists and butchers and reapers and soft-spoken peacekeepers, who are all sexually attracted to children, *short eyes*, all lumped together in there like one big stool, all complaining and sneezing and snoring and hawking and spitting and shouting and shitting and—oh god, the fury of cocks; only to be shifted from one holding cell to another, and then another and another until you are finally thankful to be integrated into a large wing where a plastic spork could peek up from a breast pocket like a pet (for after dedicating myself to the arts I've been encaged several times, twice in there although only for a few weeks; yet during those times I learned that you can *never* lose your spork, because eating oatmeal with your ass-wiping hand maybe downright degrading but you damn sure would do it). State Road: a strip of correctional facilities belying their efficacies in the northeast quadrant of this city (one of which being the wheel-and-spoke designed and designated House of Corrections), where some of its detention units accommodate close to two hundred and fifty men on two tiers inside of eight sizeable cells, four on either side of this immense warehouse of a wing divided by an open space shaped like a diamond with a guard station in the middle, with only two shower stalls and three commodes to relieve the thirty or so men in their given accommodation. No one's supposed to be in there for long though, a year the most, and once you're convicted you're transported to and processed at SCI Graterford, just west of the city, a seventeen-hundred-and-thirty-acre thirty-foot-high-walled nine-towered (manned by sharpshooters) double-gated airlocked shiny bright hell, stomaching over thirty-five hundred souls, a penal farm where various factories generate a revenue of millions while paying the prisoners peanuts, a place where a prisoner of conscience, a journalist with dreadlocks, has been paddling down the eddies of death row for over twenty-five years, and where you are asked upon arrival: Where would you like your body sent? After Graterford the second son was transported to SCI Camp Hill (not far from the firstborn), then finally over to the newly mushroomed SCI Pine Grove, to a small county on the far western side of this state (the *Christmas Tree Capital of the World,* Klu Klux Klan territory) in a grand scale effort to upscale states by providing dependable revenue, to a maximum-security prison where at thirty-two and a model inmate he could mentor youths adjudicated as adults; but before his conviction, inside of a swarming cell, State Road held him for *two* years as the judicial juggernaut deliberated postponed stalled and forgot about a lot, only to give him a minimum of ten and a maximum of twenty (this being his third smalltime infraction within the span of fifteen years)—yet all that judge had to do was to *sneeze* and the evidence would've been gone.

On State Road I've seen men beaten by women so badly, he says, that their own women would walk right pass them

212 MARC ANTHONY RICHARDSON

in the visiting room. Once when I was en route to this open-spaced visiting room he's referring to this female guard—most of the guards there are uneducated blacks—had a mother removed from line and placed inside a small room for her to undo the child's diaper, and then for her to strip herself: a regulation and yet at one's discretion, for the guard had just let another mother pass through without any provocation; and inside that air-conditioned nightmare the guard had fixed the woman's son with such presumptive disdain that, later in the lobby, she told me that the guard had been beaten barren, that she had shared the same room with her the same sorority. Of course, at their discretion, two male guards with latex gloves and aplomb would take me into a room while the second son would be taken into another: Take off your clothes, they would say to us, open your mouth lift your tongue bend spread them and cough—which felt oddly analogous to when we were being beaten as boys. Sometimes the male guard executing the directive was a latent homosexual, for one guard had to lay down his post outside the visiting room because he couldn't cope with the nightmares: people popping up in places where they oughtn't be popping up. A known homosexual was asked to search the second son once, and although his hair was often braided by men, men who love men, he was so emasculated that he would've never had the visit had not the visitor been his mother, a link to the outside, whom by another's discretion had been asked to lift up her breasts drop her pants bend spread them and cough. So when they entered the visiting room, like the currency and the take-out carton revolved inside the tiny two booths, the prisoner and the visitor were exchanged.

The female guards, boomeranging from abuses, coagulating from rapes, can be of the most vindictive stock—as well as the most opportunistic: On State Road I could've had a woman any time I wanted, the second son admits, and inside this virtual visitation room the screen is so revolutionarily clear that I can almost reach in to touch the braids of this television evangelist. There is no Plexiglas encasement nor is the camera composing my eye, perched atop his television, protected: provocation from an ill-received virtual visit would be unbridled, which makes me feel as though I am talking to a test subject in orange coveralls, contrasted by the white room and sitting upright at an unbolted-down metal table and chair to prove that the product's no further a threat. And yet not fully so. Rubbernecking is pretty common on State Road, he says; the female guards look into your books to see how much money you have, and if you have a roll they would proposition you: just last week, here at Pine Grove, I'm sitting here in the cell, right, when this woman comes in and stands right next to me and says, So what you are drawing?—mind you, a guard can *never* be alone in a cell with an inmate. (Just then, behind him, I see a face in the window on the door before it disappears.) I'm scared stiff, he says, back against the wall, sweating; I have a few hundred on my books from drawing commissions and working men's cases, so when she comes into my cell and starts asking questions and touching my arm, like this, I have to remind her of who I really am and what I really do—give Sunday services and everything. She gives me a look then and smiles as though she's sorry—mind you, this is the same woman who had another guard stomp a man into wine on steel stairs for saying something foul to her: she was servicing them both. And that man, the case I was working, still recovering from a shooting, had his colostomy bag burst. She even had me stomped for trying to stop it, and then thrown into the hole; *Mount Sinai* we call it—and here *she* is with the ovaries to ask me to pray over her...privately...I guess you can't look down on someone you look up to, because she takes the storage keys and takes me up there and it seems like she's sincere, you know, but I'm afraid of a trap: I haven't made love in so long. Yet it had just rained and I was watching the sun coming through the mesh fortifying the windows, like a web drenched in dew, lit up by the light and I was wondering about that alabaster box of ointment, about how that prostitute had anointed the Master's feet with her own tears and then dried them with her hair, about how the Pharisee had scowled at her act of love and what the Master had said, He who is forgiven much has much to love—and about whom *she* must have to forgive, if only for herself. *Forgiveness is the fragrance, she said, that the violet sheds on the heel that has crushed it.*[38]

He asks why I'm asking about this and I have to remind him of who I am, of the upcoming court hearing and there can be no more postponements: Yes yes, he says, you always had to be a little hungry. But whatever you do though, don't go in there like a guilty man. Hear me now: what is falling apart could be coming together, so I will keep the best of you, little brother, until you can keep it for yourself, a keepsake. And my eyes my eyes, Marie, I don't restrain it. After a moment I wipe them and ask him how he's been, has the firstborn visited him? He has. He talked about having gone into our house, about our father's apartment: He should have never died the way he did, he said, half-exposed. I apologize to the second son for not having gone out there this summer, for not having his daughter here today: she was seven when he went in; she'll be seventeen soon. I don't think he would even be in there if it wasn't for that officer, the one who threw him down the stairs while hall-sweeping in high school for illegalities; I ask him if he remembers the father—the one person who we thought would defend his son's innocence—taking the officer's side— and he says that even *with* that concussion he remembers…but don't be too hard on him: How many of us could have said we were tired of going to Disney World? And now look at us, I say, one of the *sons of Ham* will be laughing in the Oval Office. The window face returns and taps the door for him to turn nod and return to me. I used to fight for my time away from you, he says, now I wish we had more sand together. I say it's been running through our fingers ever since we took our plates to our television sets. Now look at us, he says, the only time we see each other is through a screen.

———————————

LOGAN CIRCLE, once a place of public execution and a grave-yard, as the sun descends I am promenading the circumfer-ence in the northwest quadrant of this city, gripping a vo-luptuously shaped paper bag to my body as the spirits burn the pockets. From its vantages, layered in winter wear, I can observe the illustriousness of its tourist attractions its places of interest, the main stem of the city libraries where I had once been commissioned, the Institute and the college and the cathedral, the Parkway flying its international colors as the symbols of assorted nations towards the Parthenon, and down the Parkway towards the thirty-seven-foot twenty-seven-ton bronze centenarian crowning the clock tower of our city hall, the tallest statue on any building on the earth: in our forefather's hand there is a gigantic scroll which when viewed from the Parkway looks as though he is engorged by a priapis-mic fury, always on the verge of delivering, but never quite. I drain and throw away the bottle and see them as I saw them in summer, the Fountain of the Three Rivers: the girl god's thigh leaning against her restless water-spouting swan representing the Wissahickon Creek, the sister god caressing her swan's neck for the Schuylkill River, and the male god a Indian brave symbolizing the Delaware, reaching behind for his bow while a large pike aback arcs a geyser gracefully above. From their mouths sculpted perimetral frogs and tortoises salute the water ballet with jets of water bursting towards its fifty-foot geyser in the center, as urchins openly rebelling the swimming ban drench themselves in laughter and watery laces of light; but these seeds are frozen now, quelled, and although everything is still covered with an aquatinted patina a thin sheet of snow lays quietly inside the forgotten fountain, mottled and pocked by the tiny stuttering footsteps of numerous fowl. For after showering this morning I wandered into the back garden and onto the thin sheet of snow as well, perforated frozen by blades of grass, looking for whom I once was, Adameve, my original state of being before experience began, before I bit the black apple. Like god walking out into the garden I walked out completely unclothed, soles burning skin smoldering—yet I was the perfect model: stuck in some indeterminate state by default, tethered by the bloody umbilical, suspended by the cryogenics of sentiment and yet moved along by the momentum of amygdalae and the smell of base fear. So that now with her having stumbled and bumped the left knee there are undertones of *amputation*, of *diabetic gangrene:* Left knee is moving, she told me, as though using herself as a metaphor to explicate my condition, when I'm moving it, she said, it lets me know that it doesn't want me to go there; left leg go numb from my behind to my foot, that's when I know it's not there, just

a piece of meat; stand still or have pain. So that now I catch
the smell and see the mouth all agape and the tongue lolling
and the teeth broken beside the buttocks, her dentures—which
she swore was done by someone else, something unseen, for
it had made an impression on her bed; I catch her eyes half-
inundated and in that half-opiate-induced tone she talks of the
tunnel, of the magnetic resonance imaging, of how wonderful
it was inside, so simple and strange, like she was in alien space
and she was so scared at first and then it was all just so simple
and strange: for last month, inside the row house, the sixth sister had died. She was found by one of her sons. The lookalike
the recluse had lost over a hundred pounds of herself to the
virus of all viruses, compliments of the common-law husband,
and had suffered some sort of failure. Although, in truth, she
had left the house long before she died.

Leaving Logan Circle, slouching towards Bethlehem to
be born, in front of a bodega aside a sewage grid gurgling
a rivulet of manhole-melted snow the snout points towards
the cesspit: freshly scissored in half (I want to leave this city; I
like this city; Dear heart, which part?) the whitish purplish en-
trails are smeared across the asphalt in a superior stroke of the
brush, an oracle of rodentia an accidental aesthetic, for where
the snout directs, there, from a fissure in thought, between the
blacken iron of the sewage grid and the unpaved pitch of the
street I will see it as I saw it yesteryear: the winter aconite's
golden cup, insidious with Cerberus's saliva and with its deeply
lobed leaves flourishing fully only once the flower has virtually
faded. But it is dark now. Midnight at six in the afternoon.
Again it has begun to snow. I insert the key card into the gate
and come upon the sedan: it will help me with the errands the
therapy, getting her to and fro. From the walkway I approach

the downstairs apartment, thinking of Andromaque and of the three of us living together, and using the spare key I open the door to enter the semi-warmth of the vestibule; the glasses fog up; I take them off wipe them put them on. Beyond the interior door I can hear the surrender of a slow drag, something about revelation by slip of the tongue or sleight of hand, and when I see myself hanging onto someone and barely moving, the raw sensuality the cling and the sway, I produce the twin pocket shots to take one—yet when I try to take the other I wretch. Okay okay, I say. Okay. I enter the living room, the same layout as above, and despite the size of its shrine, the cabinet of keepsakes, its *emptiness* forever fills me: I left a friend in a fight. Everything is essentially dark, but instead of turning on a light I move towards the illumination from within, yet balk at entering the windowless kitchen, standing at the curtainless threshold, reduced to this domain. Yet since the bed- and the bathroom doors are open so she can listen to her music, since the candlelight the only light is cast across the kitchen floor, the drag draws me nearer to where the body appears upon the bathroom floor.

I turn on the light, so many cockroaches, but I am not as terrified as I am tired. Why did you do this? I'm kneeling; you knew I was coming to wash you. She is naked, unconscious again, lying facedown in herself her water and with a new bruise at the base of her neck—and I cannot see and throw away the glasses, breaking them, in order to wipe them my eyes and lean over; with considerable effort, without thought to further hurt, I manage to turn the body on its back and when I reach for the facecloth Cupid's bow could be the crest of her upper lip, for she is shooting syllables with her lips: Mama? I kiss them and the eyes slightly open. Can you hear me? Can you move? She cannot speak anymore, she cannot move. I look down at her leg her knee—it is the size of a small head, grayish greenish and she is much much heavier than the last time I found her this way years ago. I stroke her hair—baby-soft—and tell her that I'll be back. I go into the bedroom to take off the record and take the last shot and when I return with the black pouch I lay a long white towel over the body and—without checking the glucose—prepare the insulin, squinting at the notches the needle, squinting is god—and I swear on my eyes I can feel her transference of fury and pain and maddening terror, her throes of self-birth, and I cannot cut what is being said to me into halves, I cannot go beyond what is so simple and strange and yet with the needle in the body and the plunger at the top, the syringe filled with so much more than what is vital, I pause: Son?

Beyond the gates, into the outer world, tiny descending skeletons of snow. Into the night I walk without weapons without clothes without eyes, reduced to this domain, to this simple shivering shape, for this morning, Marie, returning from the back garden naked I lay down beside your substitute, covering myself once more with her hospitality, careful as to not touch her body while mine was still cold and lying beside her I saw this psychedelic dot before my eyes and *light* shot out of my pores, the panic, yet as soon as it subsided this alarm was allayed: having been bombarded by auras, in the loosening grip of a migraine, I was once lying in *your* bed finally fucked and feeling fine and was about to fall asleep, seeing myself my seeds spilling out of you still, when you returned to my side to touch me—and in one clean motion an arm had already stretched out for a claw to grip your gullet, as the other arm was already half-cocked with a fist, yet as soon as I saw you I had released you just as quick. Now even a greater beauty is releasing *me* from *you*. Ferae naturae, you whispered, and then plunged the snout into my armpit, for without the facade of fragrances of forgiveness armpits, you believe, reveal the truest fate, them and pudendum. I remember the sometime-smell of you, strong and argumentative, but by smelling a person and only another person could *you* ascertain temperaments, dream auguries, for after three long years of reliving this city this natal city I have yet to reach the Atlantic, to witness the sun of a rising, for the reoccurring reoccurring dream of Medusa Marie is still preceding me: I give you back, you said, I give you back—and I am seeing it as you saw it taking a shot of fresh air, walking fast faster breaking into a street sprint, somebody's bare back a man's, French coffee roasted from the sun, and from the vantage of the dreamer I am chasing it hunting it weaving with it as it weaves through thick bush briers and bramble, bobbing beneath boughs to be slit-slash-slit by patterns of light and barbed shadow, and then breaking off into a clearing and into the courts of praise to sooner leap off some grassy embankment with arms stretched out wide and fruitlessly like the wings of a wild cock, flailing and falling down down and into the grace and grit of the dark red ditch: I give you back…I give you back…

ACKNOWLEDGMENTS

IT TAKES A VILLAGE: gratitude towards the Fiction Collective Two, Michael Mejia, Lance Olsen, Dan Waterman, Vanessa Rusch, and all the staff at the University of Alabama Press, for giving the book a bunker; Tessa Fontaine, the *Western Humanities Review*; the Vermont Studio Center and the Zora Neale Hurston/Richard Wright Foundation for the peacetime; Mills College, Antioch College, the Pennsylvania Academy of the Fine Arts, the Philadelphia High School for Creative and Performing Arts, the University of Pennsylvania Libraries, and the Philadelphia Libraries, for making me sharper; Micheline Aharonian Marcom, for making me deadlier; Marita Golden, Cristina Garcia, and Cornelia Nixon, for making me want more; William Scalia, Rend Smith, Shannon Mauldin, Nick Szuberla, David Font-Navarrete, Thorsten Bacon, Andy Abrams, Matt McGrath, Tamara Shulman, Vivien Carter, Mara Geller, Sarah Barab, Elijah Pringle, Mark Knight, Chris Rector, and Dana Crum, for supporting this insanity early on; Cleavon Smith, Julia Nemeth, Carolina De Robertis, Francis Hwang, Sara Campos, Scott Duncan, Wendy Breuer, Mũthoni Kiarie, Alex Kanevsky, Hollis Heichemer, Anders Uhl, Melissa Hayes, and Susan Schulman, for servicing this insanity *later* on; Hollis again, for her visceral art; Martin Campos, for his artistic push; Keleigh Friedrich, for her expansive understanding of the story; Delia Desmond and Dongshil Kim, for their loving kindness; Lovie Lee Williams, Queen Sutton, Varnnie Victor, and Cynthia Fooks, for their bottomless insight and love; Malcom Brian and Michael Corrie, for their brotherhood; Malcolm Anthony, for his vulnerability and fire; and lastly, Betty Jean, for giving me the love and the room to love us all. Àsé. And so it is.

NOTES

1. Flannery O'Conner, *Mystery and Manners* (New York: Farrar, Strauss and Giroux, 1970).

2. Molière, *Le Dépit Amoureux*, 1656, ACT V, SCENE III.

3. E. M. Cioran, *A Short History of Decay: Subterfuges* (New York: Arcade, 1998), 51. Translated Richard Howard.

4. Henry S. Haskins, *Meditations in Wall Street* (New York: William Morrow, 1940), 135.

5. Robert Henri, *The Art Spirit* (Boulder, CO: Westview Press, 1984).

6. F. Scott Fitzgerald, *The Crack-up* (New York: New Directions, 1945).

7. W. B. Yeats, "The Second Coming," in *The Collected Works of W. B. Yeats, Volume 1: The Poems* (New York: Simon & Schuster, 1997).

8. A landmark show organized by Robert Henri at the Macbeth Gallery in New York.

9. Robert Henri, *The Art Spirit*.

10. Salvador Dalí, *The Secret Life of Salvador Dalí* (New York: Dover, 1993).

11. Ambrose Bierce, *The Devil's Dictionary* (New York: Oxford University Press, 1999).

12. Theodore F. Wolff, *Enrico Donati: Surrealism and Beyond* (Manchester, VT: Hudson Hills Press, 1996), 29.

13. Jean Cocteau, *Le Testament d'Orphée*, Cinédis, 1960.

14. An island off the coast of Senegal where African slaves were held before the Middle Passage.

15. Ezekiel 37:3–6.

16. A painting by Goya.

17. The Black Panther Party for Self-Defense, which originated in Oakland, CA.

18. F. Scott Fitzgerald, *Babylon Revisited* (New York: Simon & Schuster, 1965), 226.

19. Fernando Pessoa, *The Book of Disquiet* (New York: Penguin, 2003), 11.

20. Virginia Woolf, *The Waves* (New York: Wordsworth, 2000).

21. Proverbs 18:21.

22. Anthanasian Grail Psalter, www.athanasius.com/psalms/psalms5.html#151.

23. E. M. Cioran, *A Short History of Decay: Subterfuges* (New York: Arcade, 1998), 50. Translated by Richard Howard.

24. "Beware the man of one book," Issac D'Israeli.

25. Henry Whitney, Bellows *Re-statements of Christian Doctrines: In Twenty-five Sermons* (Cambridge, MA: Press of John Wilson and Son, 1867), 149.

26. Arthur Rimbaud, *Selected Poems and Letters: A Season in Hell* (New York: Penguin, 2004), 147.

27. Kahlil Gibran, *Sand and Foam* (New York: Alfred A. Knopf, 1999), 74.

28. Charles Baudelaire, *The Generous Gambler* (1864).

29. Luke 16:24. (This is not the Lazarus that Jesus raised from the dead.)

30. Thomas Eakins, Pennsylvania Art Exhibit, *Public Ledger, January 16, 1893.*

31. Mark Edwards, *The Collected Works of J. Krishnamurti, Volume XV, 1964–1965: The Dignity of Living* (The Krishnamurti Foundation, 2012).

32. Edgar Allen Poe, "Hop-Frog," in *The Complete Tales and Poems of Edgar Allen Poe* (New York: Castle Books, 1985).

33. William Blake, *The Marriage of Heaven and Hell: A Memorable Fancy* (New York: Dover Publications, 1994).

34. The anamorphic skull is intended as a memento mori: "Remember you have to die."

35. Arthur Rimbaud, "A Season in Hell," in *Selected Poems and Letters* (New York: Penguin, 2004), 147.

36. Lawrence Durrell, *Justine* (New York: Penguin, 1985).

37. Henry David Thoreau, *The Journals of Henry David Thoreau, Volume III* (New York: Peregrine Smith, 1984).

38. Mark Twain quoting an asylum inmate.

CPSIA information can be obtained
at www.ICGtesting.com
Printed in the USA
FFHW02n1754140918
48367144-52223FF